Nate Roden

One Man, Two Countries - and Death Follows

John Jenner

Nate Roden

One Man, Two Countries - and Death Follows

John Jenner

TABLE OF CONTENTS

CHAPTER ONE
THE VAGABOND

The four men encircled each other as the terrified villagers of Mnsk gazed on. Three of the men were sizing the Outsider up for a beating as the he watched them move around. Eventually, as the Leader of the three men had intended, both of his men were standing behind the Outsider and he, the principle Leader, was standing in front. He smirked as the Outsider's full attention was now, seemingly, concentrated on him. This man wanted to be absolutely certain of the outcome of this scrap as the whole village was looking on and it was necessary that he should defeat this interloper in front of them and to do it convincingly for the authority of the Tulse Family was at stake if he did not.

As the Leader, Tito Tulse, stood still, the Outsider straightened up and took a casual stance. He thinks it will be just me and him and my two Consorts will not interfere, thought Tito. Today, he will learn a valuable lesson.

From the villagers who were grouped together, still terrified at this scrap, one woman – middle aged and beating at her chest - ran forward and grabbed her 15-year old Son, Bora, who was lying in the dirt, his face near pulped by Tito and his two Consorts. His crime? He had called Tito's Father, Zebo Tulse, a "cheap Gangster who thought he was American." Gangster, definitely. Cheap? His Father? The only man who owned outright the only four-storey Mansion in the valley of Mnsk – cheap? Well, the outcome of that child's insult was a savage beating – against three men so much older, more physically powerful than a mere teenage boy and all three armed – and Bora paid for his slight with a beating which, had it been allowed to continue, would have resulted in a bodily pulverisation from which he would probably not survive and if he did, would be crippled for the rest of his life.

And had this Outsider – this "Vagabond Stray" not interfered, that would certainly have been the case.

The curious paradox was, the Mnsk villagers were now more scared of this Outsider proving to be more accomplished against Tito than they were against him – for if Tito were to fall by this man's hands, there would be such a violent retribution led by his Father - Zebo Tulse – and his mobster Family. Many of the villagers – mostly the Mothers – begged the Outsider to flee the scene and not to involve himself any further in their personal business. The boy could be taken aside and his manners adjusted but if any of the three men – Tito in particular – were to be hurt or, Heavens Forbid, killed, the village would be razed to the ground by fire with the villagers still inside their hovels and Zebo would watch and listen to the screams with a look of dispassionate indifference for the revenge of his Son's pain, humiliation, death.

The prowling around came to a stop and for a moment, it looked as though it would be just Tito and the Outsider. Hardly a fair contest for Tito stood at six feet and was heavily muscled. His two Consorts likewise endowed. The Outsider was a smaller, older man, not seemingly particularly graced with muscular advantages and any fight against him with surely be over in minutes. What would happen to him then was also a cause for concern for the villagers. Would the three gangsters just leave the dead body here on the village street or take him, alive or dead, to the big mansion on the hill? A quick, merciful death was to be prayed for, thought the villagers as a single unit.

In the event, that did not happen.

One of the Consorts, Brko by name, the villagers knew him, stepped forward up to the Outsider's back and was about to wrestle him to the ground when the Outsider stepped aside just as Brko brought his powerful arms down on now thin air. This was followed by the Outsider striking Brko across his huge belly with the side of his hand which, unbelievably, brought the large, well-built Consort to the ground and gasping for breath.

The second Consort followed his compatriot into action and stepped forward only to be met by the Vagabond's stabbing hand, fingers straightened, striking at his throat, compromising his Trachea and sending him, like Brko, falling to the dirt ground.

Tito saw these blows and then knew this was no ordinary man standing in front of him. His already heroic though foolish interference to save the boy was an indication that he had courage and possible skills for to strike out at a much bigger man, as he had done so against Brko, would require such an attribute if he wished to live longer.

And now, with his two Consorts down, the arena was just between the Outsider and Tito. And Tito was scared. This fear was relayed in the eyes of the villagers who watched now with even more careful gaze.

Brko rejoined the fight – or attempted to – by standing and yelling at this insolent Outsider and the Outsider responded by striking him with the back of his fist across his squat nose. It was as though Brko's nose exploded, for a volcanic eruption of blood jetted out from his face and this blow was enough to end Brko's contribution to the fight. The second Consort – Sandor by name – was still choking on his compromised Trachea and blood spat out of his mouth. He would not take further action here.

And so indeed, it was just Tito and the Outsider.

For a few seconds, it appeared to be stalemate, neither man moving. Bora's Mother, Anka, saw Tito slide a flick-knife into his hand and as he opened it, he sprung at the Outsider who calmly caught the knife-hand and twisted it and Tito around until he fell on his back and the Outsider stamped on his chest with his knee taking all Tito's breath away.

The Outsider gripped Tito's knife-arm and it was brute strength against technique for the villagers could see there was no expressions of fear or fury on the Outsider's face. It was clear to nearly every villager that this course of fighting was nothing new to this man. He took Tito by the wrist and turned the arm around and now the knife in Tito's hand was pointed at him – at his throat.

Tito thrashed around like a harpooned swordfish in the ocean as it was being pulled into a sailing boat piloted by the most powerful fisherman. And even as Tito thrashed around, the Outsider slowly drew the knife closer to his enemy's throat.

The knife-point was now at Tito's throat and as he stared at it – and at the Outsider – he could see the man was just playing him. He had the strength and maybe even the inclination to push this knife into his throat and he was just keeping the tip of the knife an inch away to see Tito's reaction.

Which he got.

Tito Tulse was a coward and a bully who lived on the reputation his Father had carved out from the bloody wars and battles he had fought against equally hard men who all sought to take the lead in the valleys around Mnsk, to own whatever piece of land they had shed blood upon and all the peasants who worked the land. Zebo was a warrior to be sure but he fought those battles by leading from the front and that was why he had such a loyal following from his men – Tito, by comparison, was just the bastard offspring who believed his Empire was automatically his and at hand – for Zebo was now old and his reign would not last for many more years hence. But Tito had not earned his right to lead – all he did was get born.

And now, Tito Tulse was on his back, in the dirt, his two Consorts defeated by this Vagabond Stray and now about to lose his own life if the man did not concede. The knife-point was stabbing into his skin…

…and Tito broke.

In front of the peasant villagers, Tito begged for his life, promised this Outsider he would be allowed to live and walk away if he did not press the knife further into Tito's throat. But this Outsider knew it was a hard country and a hard life filled with hard people who led by inflicting harm and death on those who had the courage to defy them but the not the intelligence or the power. In fact, it was for exactly this reason this man was even in Albania. He was here for a purpose – and that purpose was now at hand. There was no way Tito would allow him safe passage after this humiliation set in front of so many witnesses.

He lifted his knee off Tito's chest – and briefly, Tito believed his lie had worked against the man, the fool – and he smiled. But the man had not been fooled and he brought his knee back down – hard – and all Tito's breath failed him and his physical strength – or what had been left of it – could not prevent the knife from reaching his throat. The Outsider stabbed the knife until the entire blade, all six inches of it, was inside Tito's throat. The Outsider ripped a piece of Tito's torn shirt and covered the wound and prevented the spurting blood from being seen so the villagers could not see how lethal the wound was. Tito thrashed the ground for maybe half a minute as his life drained away and he saw the darkness of death engulfing him as his senses slowly ceased and pain was no longer affecting him.

His body calmed, his breathing slowed, his reactions diminished until he lay still and he stared at the beautiful blue sky above him.

In his final seconds, a curious, non-sequitur thought entered his fragile mind. How was it, he thought, that I have never stayed still long enough to see the real beauty of this world? The country, ravaged by poverty, was indeed beautiful, the people were good and honest and tireless in their industries, the sky was clear and the air was sweet. How is it I have lived this life, now 29 years, and I have never seen it in its true light before? What a waste.

Those were Tito Tulse's final thoughts before he took his last breath and the weight of the world gently lifted from him and he was at peace – possibly for the first time in his life.

The Outsider stood up. His hands were covered in blood and the more observant elder villagers saw his clothes were also covered in blood – and not just from this fight. The blood was dried and away from where the blood had been spilled this day. His face was red from the exertions and he expelled a long breath. He stood up and the villagers saw the dirt in his clothes. Old dirt.

So, this man had clearly fought somewhere else before coming to Mnsk. He stared at the dead Tito. He confronted the two ailing Consorts who saw their Leader's Son lying dead in the dirt and knew their lives would be forfeit for this failure to preserve him. Zebo Tulse would not question them as to the abilities of his Son's murderer – that he was clearly skilled in a fighting form not common to this land and therefore a stranger, an Outsider, a Vagabond Stray. Why was he here? Zebo Tulse wouldn't even care. He had eight Sons – two Daughters - but the girls did not feature in his life as a Parent. Daughters do not carve Empires and lead armies. Sons do. Tito was his first born and to a man like Zebo Tulse, blood was all important in such a country. His Father, his Grandfather, his Family had always led the battle and today, one part of that battle was now lying dead – killed by an Outsider Vagabond Stray. Retribution must follow.

The Outsider stared down the now terrified Consorts who scrambled away. Their principle encampment was just 15 kilometres from this tiny insignificant village and their vehicle parked up at least 2 kilometres away meant their journey was going to be a long one…

…assuming the Outsider was going to allow them to live.

He turned to the villagers who now – to a woman – crossed their hands in a religious genuflection as if praying for this man to be allowed to escape his foolishness by killing the Tulse offspring. Anka stepped forward and begged him in her stuttering Albanian tongue to vacate this village at once and 'shpeto veten, i huaj.' "Save yourself, Stranger."

The Outsider nodded. He watched Brko and Sandor rushing away – as much as their limping legs would allow - but he did not pursue them. They would report this matter to Zebo Tulse and that was also a part of his purpose.

He took Anka's weathered and wrinkled hands and said 'Faleminderit' and walked away at speed. Anka took her bloodied Son, Bora, away from this hell for no boy of such an age should have to see death like this. An elder of the village brought out a small sheet and covered Tito Tulse with it – seeing the knife hilt in his throat, and gestured for everyone to now get away from this horror and get back to their homes, be ready to pack up and leave for as sure as there is God above, Zebo would be here within hours.

No-one argued against this sage's advice and all ran to their homes – with the exceptions of other boys, Bora's age, who stared at death for the first time in their short lives before being hurried away by their Parents.

One of the boys, Rado by name, was gazing at something in his hand.

It was a phone. A mobile phone. And on it was the full story image of the fight from beginning to end, starting from where Tito had beaten his friend Bora, the intruder preventing further harm to the boy and the fight between the four men leading to the death of Tito Tulse.

This phone, and its images, would be the saving of the village.

C H A P T E R 2
A JOLLY HORSE-RIDING JAUNT IN A SUFFOLK LANE

The six horse-riders took the lane very carefully as it was wide enough for a car and maybe Ramblers but only if both parties crouched into the sides of the tree growth either side of the lane. The leader of this jolly jaunt upon horse-back was Max Tierney who owned the *TIERNEY EQUINE FARM* just a few miles away and across the fields. They had all kept to the land thus far but in order to reach the Farm, it was necessary to make this detour otherwise the two-hour jaunt would be extended by an hour and he had other clients lined up for the three o'clock session. Another twenty minutes and they would all reach the Farm on time and another six horses would be lined up.

In this line-up there was only one student who could not be considered to be wholly confident upon her ride and so Max Tierney ordered the ride to be conducted along the lines of Health and Safety to prevent any un-necessary harm – much to the annoyance of at least two of the other riders.

Max took point – dressed in a black blazer, white strides, a Bowler hat and leather boots. Behind him was the youngest student in his class – Lainey Browne, 12 years of age and only with just one year's worth of horse-riding under her belt. And so, Max demanded care and consideration for his youngest charge.

Behind Lainey sat her Mother, Sasha – a former student of the same class and farm but from a different period of time. Like Lainey, Sasha had started young and was galloping her horses by the time she was 13 years. She understood Max's caution and did not press for a canter – especially on some of the terrain they had traversed the past few hours.

Behind Sasha was a young man Sasha did not particularly like and whose company she would prefer not to keep. Billy Telling, 23 years of age, the only Son of William Telling – another Farm owner and a man whose reputation was well known around Suffolk as a man not to be treated too lightly for his propensity towards active aggression came as fast as the cars he drove and with the same degree of lack of care. William Telling was one of three farmers who had bid against Tierney – a man not from these parts – and he was beyond furious when the bidding was won by Tierney. The Equine Farm was a beauty spot and a definite money-winner and Telling had campaigned both before and after the bidding to keep the Equine Farm in local hands. He lost. Unlike the other two Farmers, however, he had not taken his loss with good sportsmanship and had continued his under-the-counter-war against the Tierney's ever since.

Sasha knew this, along with many others in the Farming Community and so it was with great alarm that she learned her eldest Daughter – Tarra – was actually dating Billy Telling. It was through her request that Billy was even included on this Jaunt and Sasha made no quibble about his being there. She voiced her opinions to and about him before the Jaunt began and was roundly ignored by her Daughter and the Tierney's. The fact that Billy had sat behind Tarra's horse for most of this Jaunt was not lost on Sasha and when they had decamped their picnic on Parrot's farm, she demanded he rode behind *her* – and not Tarra. Sasha had already witnessed Billy photographing Tarra's backside and she knew he was sending the images along to his equally odious "mates".

Tarra, resigned to the walking Jaunt and her Mother's prejudice against her boyfriend, rode her mount with indifference. It mattered not to the Team Leader that she had been riding safe in the saddle for nearly all her life, having been taught to ride by her Father, Edmund, from the age of 5 years, when the Browne Family ran their own farm many years ago – a beautiful farm surrounded by nature's finest output of land and scenery and a piece of property which had been lost to the Browne Family when its Head – Tarra's Father - had been caught embezzling funds from a number of Organisations he was a Director of and had been convicted to three terms of imprisonment – but this sentence was delivered in his absence, for on the day of sentencing and knowing he was due a long spell in gaol, he took off to another country and no-one knew – or admitted to knowing – where he was currently living. Two weeks after he did the ignominious bunk, a local woman, the youngest Daughter to their nearest neighbour from the land next to the Browne's farm also fled the country and it came out that she and Edmund were in a *"loving-relationship"* – he 42 years of age, she just 23. The whole sordid affair then became a major revelation in the Tabloid Press following the embezzlement aspect and their story was played out in the few weeks which followed and Sasha was mortified in the subsequent humiliation, shunned by her upper-class "friends" who dropped her company the day the news was "leaked" and the Family was effectively dis-owned, thrown out of their once-happy Community. The upshot was the remaining members of the Browne Family was forced to sell up their beloved farm and to downgrade from their once glorious luxurious lifestyle. They now lived in a very comfortable, but very old, "Keeper's" Lodge, spacious by common standards but still a long way down from the home they had lived in. The Lodge was owned by her Father-In-Law who took pity on his Daughter-In-Law and Grandchildren. He publicly condemned his Son's actions and felt it was his duty to protect the innocent parties in this business.

And so, Tarra Browne rode behind her Boyfriend, bored witless riding at such a slow pace and was looking forward to getting back to Tierney's Farm where she could then break away from the group and take her horse for a genuine gallop across the land without being guarded by the officious Max Tierney.

The final member of the group was Max's Wife – Jean – who jealously guarded her status in the whole group and made absolutely certain no interloper could inveigle their way in and seek to diminish her role as Wife, Farm Owner, Co-Director in the Farm and Leader of Jaunts such as this one. Some had already tried, for the Farm was a genuine and profitable going concern and Max was lucky to have it, the land, *and* a Wife who knew the business better than even he did.

Just a few miles away from the Equine Farm, the jaunt took the riders down a long country lane and caution was definitely required here for local car drivers used this road like it was the Monaco Grande Prix circuit – Billy Telling being one of them…

…and as if on cue, a car – a big sporty model - came around the bend in the road. Loud, roaring.

An Aston Martin V12 Vantage sped into view and Max Tierney reined in his lead horse and raised his right hand to signify '*STOP*'. What this group did not need at this time was a thoroughly spoiled imbecile with more petrol in his head than brain cells, speeding past them at God knows how many miles an hour, frightening both horses and riders and maybe even unseating them. Accidents meant Police, bad publicity, possibly a Law-Suit… nightmare.

In the event, none of Max's fears were realised for the driver slowed the car down, reversed it back to the bend in the road and turned the engine off. The driver then beckoned with his hand outside the driver's window for the six riders to continue onwards and Max raised his hand to signify '*WALK ON*'.

Grateful for the driver's common sense and care, the riders had progressed just six yards when the driver raised his hand to compel them to stop – which they did. Max was uncertain if the driver was a comedian just playing them about or if there was a genuine reason for the emergency halt – and then he saw the blue reflection bouncing on and off against the trees and he knew at once what was happening.

The driver waved his hand out of his window to convey the situation to the oncoming emergency vehicle coming from the other end of the lane, and for them to slow down as he pointedly jabbed his hand towards the horse-riders.

The warning message was read at once for the speeding Police car slowed, turned its emergency beacon off and when it reached the bend, the driver Police Officer took the corner with great care. Her passenger indicated to the Aston Martin occupant with his thumb that another

Police car was behind them and the driver nodded. Sure enough, the second speeding Police car turned the bend a quarter of a mile down the lane and was speeding towards this situation when it also slowed, turned off its emergency flashing beacon and took the corner with great care, the Aston Martin driver gently waving and allowing the Police car to pass by him.

When both emergency vehicles were safely past the horse group, their siren lights came back on and their speed resumed and were both soon out of sight down the lane.

Max raised his hand a second time as the driver again beckoned them onwards. When he reached the car, Max – a gentleman – doffed his Bowler hat and thanked the driver for his solicitous actions.

Lainey briefly smiled to the man inside the car and said 'Thank you,' but never taking her eyes off the road ahead.

Sasha was more effusive and offered genuine thanks to the sensible car driver of a car more known for speed than gentility.

Billy raised his hand and did not speak.

Tarra was more curious for though wealth was not uncommon in these parts, to be driving this kind of car indicated great wealth and Tarra was shallow enough to be interested in anyone who possessed enough wealth to be able to purchase this kind of vehicle. She leaned forward when she was next to the driver's position and stared inside. Momentarily, she groaned, for the man was not young – well, not by her standards anyway. He was at least in his 40's, tanned, his arm, seen within his short-sleeved shirt, was muscular. Not good looking but… well, not *IMMEDIATELY* good looking but then she had such a limited CV on male relationships and comparisons were few and far between. Really, the only men she knew over 30 years were the Fathers of her fair-weathered friends and to her they *did* look old – the land and their lifestyle did that to them, she supposed. She saw him once more as he smiled at Jean – ye-es, she thought. Possibly a ruggedly handsome man – a bit like the actor who'd played a Secret Agent in the cinema that Mummy said had aged so well. Jean was equally gracious in her thanks and praised his care for the horse group.

The group had taken maybe twenty more yards down the new lane before the Aston Martin was re-ignited and quietly drove away from the bend in the lane. Tarra turned around and saw the driver smile at her. She waved but by then, he was gone.

I wonder who he is, she thought.

CHAPTER 3
THE EVENING PARTY…
AND DUCKS

The boredom of the Jolly Jaunt was relieved for Tarra when Max allowed her another hour to take a gallop across his farm land on a new horse which had not been previously booked. Tarra – sans safety helmet and restrictions – galloped *"KNIGHTMARE"* across that land for half an hour before taking him around the fields to view the other horses not on duty that day. Now she remembered the love and fun of horse-riding she'd enjoyed when she was Lainey's age and, without *loco parentis* and actual parent restrictions, she felt free.

But even here her mind was not fully on the ride.

Tarra was in a strange position. After Daddy's indiscretion with both money and female companionship, her life had taken a downward turn and instead of receiving a promised inheritance which would have kept her in society's good graces for at least another five years – she was forced to consider her future in a different way. At 16 years of age, she'd had no main ambitions to do anything worthwhile with her life, assuming her future would be sealed by choice of Husband and *HIS* occupation which would no doubt be involving a highly paid salary and a position of status she could boast about when meeting similarly positioned fellow Wives. But not now – Daddy's actions had resulted in a downgraded Browne Family home which had consequences affecting the choices for her future. She was close to leaving school so… what next?

Well, Mummy answered that. University she said. The problem with that possibility was that Tarra was no academic and school had bored her. The idea of going to a higher place of education where you would actually *NEED* to work – using your own initiative and researching books – *BOOKS???* – yeuk – did not answer her once-upon-a-time desires to live a prosperous life and putting in as little physical and cerebral effort into such matters as was possible.

And so, she went to University, was quickly bored, walked away after three years by scraping a measly 2:2 in Geo-Politics – why did she do that, she asked herself - and chose to go back-packing with three similarly unambitious girlfriends, intending to trek around the globe, have an adventure and live off the land.

She made it as far as Northern France and after the umpteenth falling out with her equally lazy fellow backpackers, decided to return home. Subsequently, apart from a few low-paid and temporary placements in manual employment where she barely distinguished herself, her once rosy-glow of her future life was now turning to dull pewter and if the only thing which can excite you is a prospective horse-riding session then your life is definitely at a standstill.

Her choice of boyfriend material emphasised her poor decision making. When they were younger teenagers, Tarra and Billy could be considered an item – at ages between 14 and 16 who really cares? – with possibly a married life beyond – but what excites a teenage girl about a young lad who frequently flexed his muscles on the sporting field - and other places, just to impress the girls - has a limited shelf-life once you've seen those muscles umpty-ump times and nearly every day. In truth, Billy was no more ambitious to improve upon his future life than Tarra was and if there was one thing of which he was absolutely certain, he knew he would *NOT* be taking over the family farm when his Father decided he'd had enough and ill health had speeded that likelihood up by some quick margin. As Billy was the only Son – both his Sisters had already fled their Family home for pastures new and foreign – it was understood by all that Billy would inherit the farm, the responsibilities and the life of a Farmer, mixing his days with other Farmers and swapping tales of hardships on how hard it is to run a farm in the 21st century.

Not for Billy Telling, that's for damn sure.

So, Tarra pondered, no life of luxury, no beautiful near palatial home, no more holidays three times a year in Monaco, Monte Carlo, Bahamas – such had been her life before *"Daddy's indis…"*

Well, *THAT* broken piece of Porcelain wasn't going to be mended anytime soon.

And Mummy was suffering as well for, like her, Mummy had been raised in wealth by Parents who'd worked for their money – something Mummy had never taken on until the financial crash of the Markets in the 1970's – and marrying Edmund Browne – a hotshot in that particular industry - was the only way out. Giving birth to two children consolidated her position in the Family manner and she presumed her life would progress along the lines of her equally fortunate fiends…

Until the embezzlement uproar and the sex scandal which followed. Then Mummy was dropped from her societal life and now they lived in a downgraded Keeper's Lodge. Thank you very much, Daddy.

She checked her watch. Time to party at the Tierney's Farm.

*

Apart from Lainey, Tarra was the youngest person at the party which was dull dull dull and the only subject of conversation from the elders was how well the children of the other party-dwellers were doing in their schools, their universities, their new jobs etc etc and Tarra smiled, falsely marvelling at everyone else's good fortune, secretly wishing she was a thousand miles away on a sandy beach and a clear blue ocean with nothing to do and no-one else to distract her thoughts.

Her thoughtful meanderings were spoiled when Billy told her, loudly, he was leaving the party because he couldn't stand to be in the company of the Tierney's any longer. The antagonism between his Family and the Tierney's was still alive and flourishing and Billy apparently intended to keep it that way. His comments were loud enough to draw him to everyone else's attention and Tarra was mortified that he'd made them directly to her – which meant that everyone at the party was now looking at her. Red-faced with embarrassment, she put distance between herself and her part-time boyfriend, and Sasha was happy to say 'Good night' to him when he asked Tarra if she was coming home with him. Arrogant boy. He left the party to the murmurings of 'Good riddance' from the twenty party-dwellers and the evening continued without rancour.

Thankfully, because of the Tierney's rigid next-day schedules, the party came to an end at eight o'clock and all made their ways to their cars and slowly evacuated the farm.

Even this parting of the ways was an embarrassment for the Browne's.

The Browne automobile was a 1975 Ford Mustang, a monster of a car far too big for Mummy to drive but as Tarra had failed her driving test three times, it was left to Mummy alone to drive the three miles to their downgraded home. Even this car was a gift from their Grandfather – another solution to assuage his guilt for his errant Son. Why he couldn't have given them a more updated and sleeker machine Tarra couldn't fathom but it was a set of wheels in a community where wheels were necessary if you needed to go from Point A to Point Z without using public transport and Mummy had a job in Bury St. Edmunds so it was a case of any car in a storm…

The drive through the lanes was pleasant and Mummy was a careful driver so Lainey had opportunity to marvel at the animals on the fields and she told Mummy and Tarra how happy she'd been seated on her horse. Sasha was happy because Lainey was happy – she being too young to understand the disgrace her Daddy had heaped on the family and as she was only 6 years when that disgrace occurred, she didn't really miss their former home, barely had any memories of it and she'd stopped asking where Daddy was and when was he coming home a long time ago. Time heals…

Two miles short of the Keeper's Lodge, they came to a stop. It was dusk anyway so vision was already limited but in this little area, the trees had grown over to form a large arch tunnel under which the driver of a car would make their way. In the middle of the road, a figure was standing and his arm was stretched outwards to prevent any further driving.

Lainey was near asleep so didn't see or feel the car slow to a halt. Tarra was apprehensive for this area was quite far away from the nearest domicile and if this fellow intended them harm, this would be the perfect spot for to do it.

'Are we in trouble?' she asked her Mother who looked equally concerned. Her hand went to her mobile phone and was ready to dial 999 if this fellow decided to cut up rough. As a precaution, she locked the car doors and had already put the car into reverse in case this man ventured towards them.

And then, they smiled. They were no longer nervous.

A waddling of ducks streamed across the road, coming from the forest on the one side and headed towards the lake on the other side. A Mother duck and six ducklings scrambled across the road and leapt onto the steep embankment, the ducklings climbing up the muddy path and entering the trees where there was a gap.

Even Tarra smiled at this.

But there was now a smaller problem – a baby duckling, far smaller than its elder siblings, sped across the road to catch them up and Mother Duck came down the embankment to assist her baby. But the kerb leading to the embankment was too high for the duckling to mount and it tried to scramble up while Mother Duck quacked her instructions to her baby as to how it should be done.

Lainey had now opened her eyes, was watching the scene and said 'Aww…' – and got out of the car.

Both Sasha and Tarra exclaimed their distress at this foolishness – who could tell what this man in the road would do – and ordered her back to the car, but to a 12-year-old girl, a stranded duckling trying to climb what must look like Mount Everest was something she needed to view close up. She ran to the place and stood in front of the man who had stopped the car.

They both stared at the struggling duckling and the Mother who was now standing above it, still quacking to her baby advice on how to negotiate the kerb.

Lainey smiled at the man. 'He can't get up the bank,' she said and the man smiled back.

He then slowly walked towards the duckling, bent down, maintained a distance from the duckling and stretched his arm out to place the back of his hand under the duckling's nether region and gently lift it up onto the embankment. It quacked and scrambled up the steep hill to join its elder siblings. The Mother Duck remained where she was and quacked at the man.

Lainey laughed. 'Is she thanking you?' she asked. The man smiled and said 'I expect so.'

In the car, Tarra was fuming. 'Goddammit,' she spat. 'How many times do we have to tell her? Don't talk to strangers.'

Sasha was about to brave the situation and removed her seat belt when the man indicated to Lainey she should return to the car by gesturing with his hand. In doing so, he stepped forward and the moon poked her brilliant shine through the tree tops. Tarra started at the man.

'Oh my God,' she said, 'that's the man we saw this morning. The one who stopped us when the Cop cars were coming.'

Sasha stared ahead but it was no use. She had barely glimpsed the man's face when she was riding her horse, being more concerned about Lainey staying atop of her mount as the Police cars passed them. The horses could easily have been spooked by the sound, the speed and the flashing lights of the Police cars and Lainey was her prime concern.

The man followed Lainey back to the car and was gentlemanly enough to stand way back from them as she climbed back into the car – apparently to give them no cause for concern.

Not wishing to appear disgruntled, Sasha leaned over Tarra's lap and said 'That was very good of you. Don't think the baby duck would have made it otherwise.'

'The Mummy duck thanked him, Mummy. I heard her.' Lainey smiled at the man, praising his action.

Tarra was more direct. 'Did we see you this morning, driving a black car, at a bend in the road? Where two Police cars went by?'

The man stepped forward and smiled. Yes, she thought, this is the same man. She looked at him. Not tall, slightly tanned, hair dark but flecks of grey in there indicating definitely he was not youth. As he smiled, lines crossed his eyes, another indication he was not youth. But he was a stranger. She knew she had never seen him around this area before and there weren't that many domiciles around The Heath that she didn't know of.

'Yes,' he confirmed. 'They were in a hurry. I actually saw where they went. Some kind of trouble on the field where a gang of lads had set a fire. The landowner had called the Police.'

Again, Sasha leaned over Tarra. 'It was good of you to make those signals – I think those Police cars would have caused a scene if they'd driven into the horses.'

The man smiled. Tarra stared at him. 'Are you from this area?'

He nodded towards the lane. 'Moved in three days ago but this is the first day I've had a chance to relax and scout the countryside.'

'Oh,' Sasha said. New people in the area were not common place and she wondered what property he had moved in to. She asked him.

'It was a derelict barn, used to be owned by a man named Haydock. I bought it six months ago and renovated the area. It's taken a while but the new house is built now and I moved in, properly, yesterday.'

Now this made sense to Sasha. She passed old man Haydock's farm area every day. He had died a year ago and his properties had been left untouched during that time while family was contacted to see how they wished the properties to be dealt with. The barn was separate to the farm – more a place to store goods and equipment, food for the animals - than an actual working area. For some time, the whole place had been covered by a high boarding and Sasha had wondered exactly what kind of work was going on behind those boarding's. Well, a new neighbour for them, for Haydock's farm was only a quarter of a mile from the Keeper's Lodge.

'Well, thank you for this morning. And for the duckling. My name is Sasha Browne, these are my Daughters Tarra and Lainey.'

The man briefly nodded – almost a bow – and said 'My name is Roden, Nate Roden. Hope to see you all soon. When we're not always passing each other.' Tarra smiled.

The conversation was over and Sasha motored on. Lainey waved at the new neighbour and he watched them drive out of sight. There was no more conversation in the remaining fifteen minutes of the drive and Lainey went straight to bed when they arrived at the Lodge. Sasha made herself and Tarra a cup of tea – and Tarra thought about the new neighbour.

Tomorrow, she thought, she would pop over to where the former Haydock barn had stood and take a look-see at this new neighbour without being in family company.

CHAPTER 4
ZEBO TULSE

Zebo Tulse stood in the middle of the street in the village of Mnsk. Every villager who lived here had been called out by his men and they had all congregated at the Cenotaph to await his fury – which was widely known to be explosive.

Zebo smiled. Something about having a reputation as being a man not to be dismissed lightly made a job like this one something to be savoured. And his reputation had been hard-earned. A man of considerable force, following on from his Father, Zelke, who had followed from his Father, Jante, as men who had ruled with iron fists and who must never be defied or betrayed.

The villagers so noted the two Consorts who had allowed that Vagabond stray to murder their Leader, Tito, and this day was the consequence of their failure. Zebo and ten men, all dressed in black suits or black leather coats arrived in a number of cars and sentries had closed all entries and exits into the town. All the men were armed and not one villager dared make a protest. In the middle of the Cenotaph area, having been pulled out by one of the black-suited men stood Bora and his Mother, Anke, who despaired at this action, fearing this would the day her Son would die.

But even before the questions were asked regarding the details of what had happened the previous day, Rado stepped forward and waved his mobile phone at the one man who appeared not be violent. And in fact, Rado's action and choice was correct for this man was the public voice of the Tulse Family – the reasonable negotiator who would speak on behalf of the Family before any unpleasantness would take place. Rolfe Tanka had all the intelligence and wiles of the first-class Lawyer and had been trained, via the Tulse Empire's finances, to serve the Family in such matters. Rado had seen this man was the Family mouthpiece and attracted the man's attention immediately by waving the phone. Tanka duly paid attention to the boy and Zebo looked on. Tanka then whispered to Zebo who nodded his affirmation. The man and the boy then entered the family home along with his terrified Parents and were there for some considerable period of time.

And while they waited, Zebo nodded to one of the black-suited men who carried a sawn-off shotgun. The man walked to where Zebo stood and gave him the shotgun. He checked to confirm it was loaded and then closed it. Zebo walked around the small dirt village square and twirled the shotgun as if it were a revolver pistol. Then, abruptly, he adopted a stance and aimed it at some of the ten men in his employ.

Not one of them moved. Had they done so their employment would possibly be forfeit. Zebo then continued his promenade only this time towards the villagers – who did not possess the stoicism displayed by the ten men – and as Zebo repeated the same action, many of them either squealed in fear or cowered backwards. Zebo smiled – there was no shame in demonstrating fear, he knew this and so did not chastise those poor villagers.

Zebo stood, deliberately or by chance, next to Bora and Anke but said nothing. They, for their part, were too terrified to protest this move and also said nothing.

Zebo scanned the group for the first time and even recognised a member who had, at some time in the past, served him or his Father. Elder…? Jono. That was the man. He had been on friendly terms with Elder Jono. He had not in the violence business but had served in softer areas of servitude. He – unlike his neighbours in the village – did not gaze upon Zebo with fear on his face but of the understanding that Zebo had committed himself to a rather unusual act today for he had barely left his mansion home in Tirana in the past ten years. Fear of assassination – for even the most feared man has enemies who are willing to place their own lives at risk by murdering someone in full public view – fear of abduction, his worst fear, fear of betrayal from within his own camp under the "out-of-sight-out-of-mind" system.

More realistically, Zebo maintained a limited period of life outside the Tirana mansion because of failing health. Now a man in his mid-70's, he was prosaic enough to know that if caught in a gunfight too far from home he would not stand much of a chance. An external attack would see him and his Band seriously compromised. At home, his mansion-cum-fortress was equipped to repel any external rampage and contained many a get-a-way facility in case the walls were broached. The elders of the village were well aware of his oft dictated dictum about trusting enemies – there was never a problem there because they were enemies and therefore he always knew where he stood with them. 'It's my friends who need watching,' he once told Elder Jono.

Tanka came out of Rado's home and walked straight to Zebo, Rado in tow, and showed the filmed contents to him. And here, in front of the two hundred plus villagers, Zebo Tulse watched on the mobile phone exactly how his Son met his death at the hands of this vagabond stray. He requested it be played back twice so he could assimilate everybody's actions in the fight.

When he concentrated on his Son's actions, he spat in disgust and muttered 'For shame' for Zebo had never ever used his position to exhibit violence purely because he could or for the fun of it and it was clear Tito was having fun beating on the poor boy simply because of an insult against his Father – such a slight is to be ignored, not treated as if it were something to be afraid of and it proved to Zebo that Tito would never inherit his mantle of Leadership – he did not have the wisdom or the humility to be a true Leader.

After he'd watched the fight for the fourth time, without barely making a specific movement to alarm anyone, he casually stretched out the hand which held the sawn-off shotgun and without aiming, blew Sandor's head off his shoulders. The luckless Consort was standing just six yards away from Zebo and was miserably looking at the ground, out of fear of how Zebo would react. At least he had not seen his impending death.

Brko did, however, and he dropped to his knees, sobbing, begging Zebo not to kill him. Zebo took the phone and ordered Tanka to pay the boy a sum of money – an amount of money than any villager would ever earn in their entire lives. Rado gratefully received the gift and he and his Mother departed at haste to ensure they would no longer witness any more violence.

The villagers – including the Elders – had all reacted in terror at this casual act of violence. There had been no indication of it about to happen. Zebo had not reacted angrily at what he had seen on the phone's images. He ordered Brko to be taken to the only vehicle amongst those they had all arrived in which did not look as if it belonged to the convoy. Zebo would deal with this gutless Consort later and at the mansion. Temporarily placated, Brko walked to the vehicle in the company of a man just a day before he would have called 'friend' but now would not even speak with him. He climbed into the back of the car and waited as the former friend re-joined the group. At this point with that group standing at least thirty metres away, Brko contemplated the idea of sneaking out of the vehicle which was parked overlooking a cliff and escaping down the side of the mountain. He could move fast when terrified and if he did it with stealth, he may succeed. He watched them for a while as they all grouped together in discussion, sidled over to the passenger door, out of sight of the group and pulled the lever to open the door…

…too late did he see the wire attached to the handle and…

…the explosion tore the car apart leaving only the chassis holding the now shredded vehicle together. Again, the villagers recoiled in terror. Even some of the ten men jumped for they had not been warned about this part of the day's plans. Only Zebo and Tanka held their nerves and barely gave the destroyed vehicle a second glance.

Tanka ordered the small army to return to their cars and wait for their Patron to come.

Zebo then did a strange thing. He went to Bora and Anke, smiled at them and said, 'How was that for a cheap American gangster?' Bora, bruised and face swollen from Tito's disgraceful thrashing, held his gaze into Zebo's face for if there was one thing he had learned about this man, it was never to show fear no matter how terrified you were.

In response to this courage from a mere child, Zebo took the boy's face in his hands and kissed both cheeks. He then spoke directly to Anke. 'This boy is now under my protection. He will never be harmed again, you have my word.' Anke, grateful for this release, then took Zebo's right hand and kissed it, blessing him for his understanding and wisdom. Zebo nodded to Tanka and the Lawyer pressed an envelope into her hands and smiled.

The two men returned to their car and got in. Zebo was still gazing at the mobile phone images. The convoy, led by the vehicle driven by Zebo's chauffeur, drove away, sending up clouds of dust and dirt. Not one villager left the area until they saw the last of the convoy disappearing over the mountain range. Only then did they breathe out great sighs of relief – they were all still alive and their day would continue as normal…

…depending on what exactly could be done about the near headless Consort who lay on their dusty street square and the destroyed car with shreds of the other dead man inside – and who would be doing it?

CHAPTER 5
THE FURY OF MUMMY'S

Three days after the 'Jolly Jaunt' and the Tierney party, Sasha received a visitor in the form of an old "friend", Annaliza Beddoes, once a member of Sasha's "in-crowd" pals who had dropped their friendship the same day Edmund's indiscretions had been made public. Annaliza, herself a person of a three-times-wedded history, had stayed out of Sasha's perimeter ever since so the visit, unannounced, came as quite a shock to Sasha and Tarra - who was in the main living room on a computer and searching for employment – something Patrice, Annaliza's eldest Daughter, did not need to do.

Surprised by the visit, Sasha allowed Annaliza entry into the Lodge – and immediately, almost instinctively, Annaliza gazed around the home and did all but wrinkle her nose in disgust.

'Nice,' she conceded. Sasha ignored the slight and waited. Tarra hadn't seen Annaliza in some while, nor Patrice, and so enquired as to how her old friend was doing.

'Oh, Patrice is doing fine,' Annaliza bragged, almost a glowing in her voice, 'working in the City. God knows where she got those brains from – it's all about number crunching apparently.'

And Sasha waited. After an awkward pause, Annaliza began.

'You're a friend to the Telling Family, aren't you? William Telling.'

'Well, hardly a friend – but I know him.' Sasha was curious now for she knew there was no love lost between the Beddoes Family and the Telling's. Was Annaliza about to request a favour for the two Families to become somehow acquainted?

Annaliza did not hesitate to state her business with Sasha.

'You know that vicious little sod of a Son of his, don't you?' said Annaliza. It wasn't asked as a question and now Sasha was even more curious. She wondered if young Billy had been setting his eyes upon Patrice – a young woman of some considerable beauty and, if the local gossip was true, about to inherit from a wealthy Grandfather not long for this world. Billy, no pauper to be sure but greedy and would swap his allegiances in a heartbeat if he knew there was something in it for his own needs. Any road out of this area and away from farms.

'Yes,' said Sasha, 'I know Billy. We are *definitely* not friends.' If Annaliza wanted Billy's kind of acquaintanceship with Patrice then she must be desperate.

But that wasn't the purpose of the visit. Annaliza went into some detail about why this visit was happening. The day before, she and her youngest Daughter, Phillipa, had been on their own horses, riding around the village, and Annaliza was already apprehensive about this trip. In the countryside, away from the snarls of road traffic, Phillipa and her mount were both at ease but coming into the village streets, Annaliza could see both rider and mount were less confident.

And Billy Telling's loud arrival only made matters worse.

'You know he's got one of those sports cars,' said Annaliza. 'A red MG type machine. Thing. Well he was speeding about the streets and when he saw us he U-turned the damn thing around and sped right past us, twice, blowing that damned horn of his. I mean, have you ever heard it? Bloody racket it makes.'

Tarra knew – she'd been in that car and Billy was a holy hellion when driving it. In the narrow lanes he was pure danger – but his desire to boast about his automobile did not fade when driving it in the village of The Heath and that included both speed and the 'damned horn' – which really did make a racket as he had had the speaker amplified and at two in the morning, the residents of The Heath would be treated to Billy Telling's loud advertisement of a car.

'Well,' Annaliza continued, 'he went past us – must have been doing bloody 90mph and it threw Phillipa's horse into a panic – I mean the mare is only young and Philly is only 12. Poor girl doesn't know how to handle a scared horse.'

'Oh my God,' said a genuinely concerned Sasha, 'she wasn't thrown, was she?'

'No,' said Annaliza and she had calmed down a bit though anger was still in her voice but now feeling she had found a potential ally in her former friend. 'Luckily, she held onto the horse and this man – total stranger - came rushing across the street and steadied her and Philly. Nice chap. He'd been jogging.'

Inwardly, Tarra was furious. This business was not just Billy being a show-off for she knew Annaliza was a close friend of the Tierney's and had been partly involved in their taking over the Equine farm as it was upon her recommendation to the previous owners that Jean in particular was an astute business person who had successfully ran similar businesses in Wales and Ireland and could be trusted to run the Equine farm in the same way. William Telling may well know how to run a farm but using it as an extra leg of business was another matter and that was why he wasn't the lucky winner of that bid. Billy's actions, driving around Phillipa's horse in such a manner wasn't just a boy showing off his toy – he was getting at Annaliza who had given her loyalty to outsiders to this community.

Which is one course of action a person may take where there is conflagration between neighbours but do not involve a child at all and especially if she's mounted upon a horse, neither being wholly confident to deal with the sudden noises on the streets. Without being asked by Annaliza, she stepped up to the plate.

'I'll be seeing Billy this evening,' she told her former friend's Mother, 'and I'll have words with him. Not pleasant words either.' Now that was enough for Annaliza to hear and she breathed out. Not that she wished to rekindle old friendships but Tarra, she knew, was the known 'item' in Billy Telling's circle and it was really to Tarra whom Annaliza was targeting her comments and now Tarra had come through. Job done. The next twenty minutes between all three was basically idle gossip-mongering and time passing. It felt odd for both Mothers to be speaking to each other like this after so long a time had passed, especially given such scandalous circumstances and, under the en clair conversation, there was a deep sense of unease between the pair of them. Satisfied she had accomplished her principle task, Annaliza made her excuses and left to collect Phillipa from school. Tarra and Sasha waved her away – and then Tarra spat, furiously. 'I'll bust his damn balls for this. A bloody child! What the hell was he thinking of?'

They went back inside where Sasha continued with her domestic duties and Tarra resumed her job search. Then – out of the blue – she said to her Mother, 'I wonder who the jogging stranger was.'

And when she said it, it suddenly occurred to her to take a walk to where old Haydock's farm barn used to be and take a look at Mr Roden's home.

CHAPTER 6

WILLIAM TELLING'S VISITOR

William Telling grunted his way through twenty minutes of heaving bales of hay from one part of the farmyard to another, some of it going on the tractor and some of it going into the barn. Billy was supposed to be assisting him but put a bit of manual work in front of that lazy sod and dynamite won't blast him out of that bathroom as he makes himself look pretty for the night out ahead.

He picked up the last but one bale, carted it across the yard, dumped it on top of the pile which was going to the barn and turned to fetch the last bale when he was saw a face peering over the yard gate. He stared at the stranger and wondered if the man was lost or if he was just curious about a farmer's duties in the yard. The man was staring *at* him – and then he averted his gaze to stare at the MGB Red sports car Billy had parked up ready to take out tonight. He was seeing that Browne girl – again. God alone knew what he saw in her 'cause she was as dull as cow piss and there couldn't be enough Gods in all of Heaven to figure out what the hell she saw in him, for, physical attraction aside, William Telling was honest enough to know his Son had all the personality of a turnip. He was all flash, a *"drive-at-90-mph kind of flash"*. He had no conversation unless it was about him and how he wanted to live in another country where there were no farms. 'Farms is where the country lives, you ungrateful little runt,' Father Telling told his Son years ago, 'an' if it weren't for us Farmers, country'd go down the cesspit. You'll learn that soon, boy, or you'd better 'cause if you don't, when you be running this farm, you'll put it on the death heap.'

If there was a moment to signal Billy's total lack of interest in farming, that was it. William Telling was a man in his late forties, and he looked like a man about to step into a coffin – the business had aged him to such a point, Billy would listen to the old man grunting and groaning his way to breakfast at four in the morning and he knew that was *NOT* how *he* intended to age.

William turned back to take the last bale and the man was still staring at him. 'I help you?' he asked the stranger. The stranger spent a few seconds in thinking up a reply and then asked, 'Is this the Telling Farm?'

William dropped the bale of hay and stared at the man. He knew he didn't know him – the area was limited to neighbours and he knew practically everyone within a five radius – and then most of the people outside that radius. He did not know this man. 'Who are you?' he asked. The man had placed both his hands on the top of the yard gate. This time, the expression on his face was not neighbourly or pleasant or friendly.

'Are you William Telling?' he asked.

William crossed the short distance and walked to the gate. 'I'm William Telling,' he confirmed. 'Who are you?'

'My name is Nate Roden. I moved into Haydock's farm a few days ago. Just a few miles away. Do you know it?'

William cursed under his breath because the store barn was another piece of property he had put in a bid for and was told another person – another bloody outsider – had secured the sale. Bloody strangers, he ranted, moving into our community. It'll be bloody Rolls Royce's and swanky hotels next. Nobody listened. The barn had been a rundown eyesore for a long time and everybody knew it, nobody would miss it if it was pulled down which is exactly what William wished to do, then build his own property there. Hopefully, the new incumbent would build something interesting there, they all said. All William knew was the land had been going cheap and yet another source of property had been denied him. He confirmed he knew Haydock's farm.

The stranger – Roden, was that his name? - wasn't he a French artist or something? – then asked if the MGB was his car.

'Mine. I bought it. I done it up so that it runs. My Son do drive it more'n I do though.'

And at that point, this Roden character gripped the top bar of the gate and fair vaulted over the top of it – didn't even have to use his feet to give himself extra impetus. Just cleared the gate – at least five feet high - and landed on both feet. Instead of even looking at William, Roden walked to the car and around it as if he were valuing it.

'What's it worth?' he asked.

William was getting a tad irate with this insufferable questioning. Who the hell do he think he is, just leaping into my bloody farmyard like he owns the place and now he's talking to me about my bloody car like we is friends

'Around £17,500,' he replied and this was an accurate answer for he had already enquired about its possible sale – Billy either could either buy his own car or he can learn how to drive a tractor. Out of pure funk, he told the stranger, 'It ain't for sale.'

This man Roden then walked around the car again and without even looking at William said, 'Wasn't thinking about buying it. I was thinking of using a sledgehammer on it. Smash it to smithereens.'

Now this is aggression and this is right up my street, thought William. This man is trying to have a go at me and I don't know why but if anyone going to be using sledgehammers, it will be me and this man can be the first to find out what it's like to be up against a toughie like myself. He put his hands on his hips and continued the man's threat.

'An' why would be doing that, stranger?' And now the stranger stood still, placed his hands on his hips and stared at William.

'Because I saw your Son, Billy, driving this menace yesterday and he almost took a young girl off her horse. And it was no accident. He did it deliberately. Even drove down the road a piece and came back to do it again. The girl is just a child. Damn near scared her to death.'

Curse you, Billy, William thought. I say give these people a reason to be scared but don't take our fight to the kids. He knew Billy had used the car to frighten a couple of horse-riders because Billy had bragged about it – scaring the Beddoes woman, he had told his Father - but he didn't know one of them was her bloody kid.

And then this Roden fellow strolled up to William and, not taking his eyes off him, said 'And after I've smashed the car to smithereens, I'll use the sledgehammer on your Son's face.'

It was here William gave serious thought not to actually lay harm upon this man for, at close range, he suddenly looked like a man who could not be intimidated, threatened or physically be pushed around – not without inviting a response – and William, hard as nails once upon a long time ago, knew he was no longer the force he once was. There was something in Roden's eyes which told William his very life could now be in danger.

He tried reason. 'Roads is for cars. Not people casually walking, or riding horses, bikes an' that.'

Roden measured the remark with 'These lanes weren't built for motor cars, not cars that go at such speeds. And everybody uses these roads. Your Son is a thug and he enjoys scaring people. I don't like that. Tell him.'

William considered clouting the man while he was still unprepared. There was a sledgehammer hereabouts. I can still swing it. Take him by surprise.

Instead, he reverted to type. 'If you don't leave, I'll call the Law.' It was all the threat he had at his disposal. Roden smiled and stepped back. 'I'll wait,' he said. He puts his hands in his pockets and stood still. William was out of threats and insults. 'I'd like you to leave now,' he countered and hoped this bastard had had enough.

Roden smiled. 'Tell your Son', he said, 'if I ever see him driving about these lanes at those speeds again, I'll haul him out of the car and I'll ram it right up his ass.'

Roden then walked back to the gate. For one moment, it looked as if he was about to repeat the same leap over. Instead, worse, he smiled at William, nodded towards the gate and said, 'Open it.'

William stood rigid. Being bloody ordered about by an interfering stranger – in my own bloody yard? Who does he damn well think he is? But after a few moments of scared rigidity, he walked to the gate, brought back the large padlock and the gate opened. Roden walked through it and then away down the lane and didn't even look back.

William stared down the road for as long as it ran – about quarter of a mile before it turned a bend and the stranger was out of sight. And then, as if timing was involved, Billy arrived and stood next to his Father. He smelled of oils and perfume and his hair was still wet.

'Who was that?' he asked.

William turned to his Son and heir and scowled. The little sod must have been watching the incident from upstairs and didn't consider to come down to address the stranger's ire himself. Bloody flash and gutless, that's my Son, William told himself.

And so he told him. The man's name, what the man said about his driving the day before and what the man said he would do if he came into contact with Billy again.

Billy scoffed – nobody would dare threaten him and William walked away. As he did so, and without turning back to speak to his Son, he said 'You may be Cock of the walk in this field, Son – but another bird has just moved in. Better watch your step.'

William stormed into his house and slammed the door. He heard Billy run up the outer metal staircase to go to his own bedroom. An hour later, he heard the MG revving up and being driven – at speed – out of the yard. Yes Son, thought Billy, you learn the hard way. Think it will happen soon.

He wondered who the hell Nate Roden was.

C H A P T E R 7

A PUBLIC SLAP IN THE FACE

Billy sauntered into *The Keys* pub after publicly announcing his arrival by the familiar and tedious blaring of that car's horn. The pub was only half filled and half of those groaned and the other half, those under the age of 21 years laughed…

…well, not all of them laughed.

Billy entered the pub and in seconds a half pint of bitter was placed in front of him. This half pint would take him at least two hours to consume because if there was one thing Billy did not foul up on it was drink-driving. His cousin, Warner Telling, had done so and he'd been caught. Points on the license, a possible driving ban and a Fine – all unsavoury elements of activities which future reviews could adversely affect him, from possible employers, possible journeys to countries like the USA for instance which don't like foreigners entering their country who have criminal convictions could impede his intended upwards mobility lifestyle. A half pint from his mates – to whom he duly returned the favour by standing his round – was all he required to enjoy the night.

He sipped twice from the half pint glass and scanned the bar. Nice looking girls in tonight so… if *she* isn't in tonight… ah no, there she is and looking very delicious. Tarra was an agreeably looking filly – not the best he'd attempted to bed – but someone who had the potential to stand as a trophy wife when communing with others of the '*Jet-set*' – that Company of '*Go-getters*' young Billy Telling had such an ambition to become a part of. And once there, he could always fish around for other future potential trophy wives if Tarra didn't share his particular ambition.

But for tonight, here she is and looking positively yum – in front of his mates who shared his ambition – *and* his lust towards Tarra Browne – and all waiting in the wings to see him muck it up with her so that any one of them could leap in and assume his position.

He was aware of his beauteous prize and how much all his mates envied him and wished to take it away from him but he knew his position was unassailable. Tarra Browne was his and here she is coming towards him… and…

WALLOP!!!

As greetings go, this slap across the face was unexpected and it bloody hurt. She had walked up to him, the expression on her own face was benign, nothing to indicate anger or fury, no warning words to express dissatisfaction or maybe even something along the lines of *"Could we step outside, dearest heart, I would like to a have a private conversation with you."*

Nope, just an approach from the front and a right-handed cross across his left cheek. The stinging slap left its imprint – a bright red hand mark across his pale un-tanned cheek, the look of total astonishment on his face and the near uncontrolled delight on the faces of his mates who wondered just what the hell had got the divine Tarra hot and bothered tonight. A common occurrence from someone who is nearly always defending herself, being always on the back foot on account of her Father's lack of discretion – a temper some of the customers had seen before - but not quite as public as this example. What on Earth…?

And nobody asked that question louder than the wounded Billy Telling. 'What the hell was that for?' he demanded to know.

And in front of the eighteen customers in The Keys, Tarra berated his actions a few days before when he had driven like a maniac near a skitty horse which had a 12-year child on its back. Not just the skid driving but that bloody horn sounding off as if the damn car was leading a charge against a foreign power armed to the teeth with weapons.

Her tirade lasted but moments and Billy – thoroughly humiliated – took her aside and apologised profusely. Not a single word was of genuine contrition and Tarra read him like the open book he truly was. She scolded him a second time – quieter this time – and by the time he'd explained his lack of driving care a third time, tempers had calmed down. They returned to the collective fold and the evening passed by relatively soundly and without further rancour. But Billy Telling would remember those few moments of humiliation – and the stinging slap – for a long time to come. As the evening drew to a close and the Landlord called 'Time', Billy casually dropped the name of Nate Roden into the conversation with his mate.

Now, none of his mates had ever heard the name before and Tarra was about to announce she had met him when another of Billy's mates intruded and asked why he wanted to know. Billy then related the brief meeting between this man Roden and his Father – and the threat which went along with the visit.

This threat enraged the mates – even more than Billy – and they all wondered aloud how they should deal with this newcomer who threatened their neighbours. Where does this man live, they asked?

Everybody in the pub knew Haydock's farm, and how it used to look. They all agreed it was a miracle that old barn had lasted so long but practically no-one knew what was standing there now.

Farmer Wilbur threw his ten pence in. 'Must be a big construction,' he said, 'on account of them large boarding's which hid the bloody place. I heard a lot of construction going on there but you can't see a thing less'n you got a cherry picker or a ladder you can scramble up on and look over.'

Is the new neighbour a farmer, rich, foreign, British, local, an outsider? All these questions were thrown at Farmer Wilbur and he shook his head in a negative response to each of them.

Only Tarra kept her silence. This man Roden had demonstrated his kindness that day by being patient and practical with the horses and the Police cars and again, later on, when he assisted a baby duckling up a steep kerb so it could join its siblings. He smiled when he was stood by their car and he seemed pleasant enough to talk to when her mother addressed him. Not aggressive or violent, so…

…either Billy was lying or Mr Roden was something else.

The thought occurred to her to maybe pay a casual visit to Haydock's farm and see if she couldn't strike up a bond of conversation with Nate Roden.

The same thought occurred to Billy Telling – and his mates – but conversation was not on the menu.

C H A P T E R 8
THE SHQIPTOSE

Zebo Tulse waited inside his mansion for the arrival of three men who had been invited to come to his home. Such an invitation was rare and one which would never be refused. Their arrival was scheduled for 20.00 hours and Zebo knew they would arrive at exactly that time. He enquired to his Counsellor if the film projector was set correctly and had it been run earlier that day? Rolfe Tanka assured him that all was set and ready for the three visitors to watch, listen and engage in the converse Zebo was to lay upon them. There was knowledge to be learned and he was curious to learn if they were also aware of his Son's death

At exactly 20.00 hours three cars were heard being escorted up the long drive lading to Zebo's home. He stood by the large window and watched as his own men stood by each car, four per car, none of them armed for these visitors would be treated with the highest respect by the soldiers who served Zebo. As a mark of equal respect, none of the three visitors had brought along with them any of their 'Family' and none of them were armed. They were on home ground and it was an understood unwritten rule that no violence and no blood would flow on home ground following an invitation to convene. This was to be a meeting of four of the most powerful men in hidden Albania and all respect would be observed.

The oldest of the visitors – in fact, the oldest of the group – was Devishi Bartok. Age did not convey automatic rights to lead – only demonstrated power from an individual achieved that Right and while Bartok was indeed a powerful man, he did not seek to rule over all. He stood still while the other two men alighted from their own cars.

40

The youngest of the four – Marku Kursk – scanned the whole of Zebo's property and scowled. How could a man who had no visible means of income live in such opulent luxury? To him, advertising such wealth was bound to bring the owner's wealth into question should a man of equal power but on the side of the Law ever come to their attention and ask that very question.

Marku was more direct in his accumulated wealth. Many of his businesses were all legitimate and he even paid taxes on them – something not approved of by his fellow Captains of misrule. Why give a corrupt Government the sweat off your own back, they asked him? His answer was always the same. In twenty years of his 'alternative' industries, he had never once been visited by the office or the Law, even though payments had been made by all four of them to ensure such attention was not paid to them. He preferred peace and quiet and tax paying was no trouble for him.

The third man was the most fiercest of the four men, with a reputation truly and hardily earned - originally a street fighter of vicious repute – he had been incorporated into the ranks of one of the 'Families' by a powerful gangster named Oscarr Gorovitch. This had occurred when that gangster had been attacked by a would-be rival who had already successfully slain three of Gorovitch's bodyguards. He had then turned his attention to Oscarr himself, who had been seriously wounded and he feared he would die this day until the street fighter intervened, even taking a bullet, and then bettered the would-be rival by constantly pounding his head against the wall. His reward was to be adopted by the Gorovitch Family. Such was his gratitude he took the Family name and even renamed himself Oska out of respect and honour of his Mentor.

Rolfe Tanka approached each man with a small bow and gestured for them to follow him.

The greeting inside the house was no less warm and welcoming and Zebo made absolutely certain each of the men were made comfortable and supplied with food and drink.

These men rarely met as they all lived in far away and separated areas of Albania. They had all reached the ages where the activities of their younger selves could no longer play a major part in their lives now. So, rarely did they meet and only when extreme business was to be discussed - such as an outside threat which could bring them to oblivion.

Once the familiarities had been dispensed, they all sat in the large lounge and the first thing the three visitors saw was the film projector set up in the middle of the room and the large screen near the wall. So – a film was to be viewed.

Before that however, Zebo turned to them and suddenly announced his Son, Tito, had been killed recently. Not just killed but beaten to death by an outsider. 'A vagabond,' Zebo announced.

To Rolfe Tanka's eyes, the resulting looks of horror on each of the faces of the three men were too genuine to be faked and he concluded Tito's death – and the manner of his death – had come as a great surprise to them. Each man then paid their respects by holding Zebo and kissing him on each cheek. Their remorse was not feigned. Among these men of power, the loss of family under such circumstances was to mourned.

'Is this why we are here?' asked Bartok. Zebo confirmed it was and he nodded to Tanka who asked the men to be seated and watch the film.

The lights were doused, the projector turned on. What was on the large screen was the same images stored on the mobile phone belonging to the Rado boy. Science had allowed a genius to transfer the images from that tiny machine to this film projector for these men of business to view – and be shocked by.

And shocked they were. They watched the film, the fight, how this Vagabond combatted the Bodyguards, then how he dealt with Tito. For the purpose now of observation, Zebo ran the film three times more so the visitors could see the face of the Vagabond who had slain his Son. He ended it the sequence on a freeze frame which gave the killer's visage image full attention.

Bartok spoke first. 'Not young,' he said, 'Mid-forties - not one of us. Not from this country.'

Gorovitch agreed and gave his opinion. 'Not a casual, Zebo – this man… fight… as a professional. He is not intimidated by the presence of the two bodyguard and his eyes never leave your Son when they joined. See how easy he deal with them. He has killed before.'

'An assassin,' spoke Kursk. 'Paid to kill Tito?'

Zebo nodded here and there but held his counsel on opinion as to why Tito was killed. It was something he had already entertained because people who behave the way Tito did are bound to make enemies. If this thing had happened in the city of Tirana he would have believed it in a heartbeat. But Mnsk was a small insignificant village, miles from any place of any importance and populated with peasants who farmed, or worked in dirty factories, or just sitting on their porches waiting to see how life would treat them that day, and then die of old age as they sat. Tito had not made any announcements of where he was going that day, that much had been confirmed by the two now dead Consorts. Either this meeting between the killer and Tito was very well planned – by someone else - or it was pure coincidence. But the fact his three visitors had agreed with his own conclusion that the killer was a professional – and a professional assassin – had some significance. It took time for each man to think about who could set this fight up – and who would have the courage?

Suddenly, Bartok became alert. 'Vanna,' he shouted. 'Edon. Vanna Bashkim's bastard Son.

A slow and long pause followed. Zebo studied the freeze frame on the screen and scowled. 'This is not Edon,' he claimed and was disappointed in Bartok's assessment.

Bartok stood and clasped his hands together as if he were excited to share details of something only he knew and the others were currently in ignorance.

'Two day ago,' he went on, putting up two fingers and almost breathless now. 'Two day – Edon and three of his fellow were confronted by mystery man who tell them to not go further into town they were entering. Edon make this fuss – "Who are you" he demand, "to tell me to do or not to do…" and then' – Bartok gestured with both of his hands to signify his point – 'KABOOM…'. He waited for the expressions on their faces to die down. Clearly, they did not know what had happened to this man, Edon.

'His head,' Bartok continued, 'Blow to pieces. Almost lose it from his shoulders. He fall – his fellow all take to hide themselves. The mystery man – he disappear.'

They all resumed their seats and now Zebo was all interest. The man Bashkim was no friend of his – very much an opponent in fact – but such a death…

'Explosion?' queried Kursk.

'Is strange,' said Bartok. 'For there is no sound. It happen just the way I say. Nothing – and then his head is gone.'

Silence followed the description and only Gorovitch had something to say about it.

'Who tell you this thing?' he asked. Discussion then followed about the three men who were with Edon at the time of his death. One of the men had dived to the ground near where Edon lay and listened. Bartok then relayed what this man had told him. There was a sound, a small kind of explosion he said, but it had come after the head exploded, not before.

Gorovitch smiled. He turned to Zebo and said, 'Sniper.' Zebo nodded. And if the sound came after the death then the sniper must have been some distance away. What the man had heard was the echo of the weapon being fired. At least two miles, Gorovitch told him. The mystery man who had stopped Edon and his friends from their walk into town had effectively set him up so the sniper did not have to aim from such a distance at a moving target.

Zebo listened to both men with interest. 'Where did this happen, Devishi? What town?'

'Was Vranks. Many mile from Edon hometown. Away from there, around the town, is mountain and tall buildings. The sniper could be anyplace and never be seen.'

Zebo knew Vranks – it was situated in the country and on the edge of a growing town. Yes, a sniper who knew his craft could take refuge in that environment and never be identified. He could hide either in the mountains where many criminals took refuge from the Law – or other criminals – and never be found in the labyrinthine tunnels which permeated the mountain range. The high-rise buildings offered equal protection.

'Edon had many enemy,' continued Bartok. 'Even his own Father hate him. But he - powerful man – powerful allies. Bashkim is sick and old – but he is not us, Zebo. He may think of Edon plotting against him…' He opened his arms out wide as if to ask the question. Could a Father – even an unrecognised Father – have his own son assassinated?

If he wished to continue his position as a man of power and reject all opposition – yes.

Zebo looked at the freeze frame again. If this man who had killed Tito was also the assassin of Endo Vanna – could he have been hired by…

'We must speak with Bashkim,' he said. 'Today.' It was a command.

C H A P T E R   9
SPYING ON THE ENEMY

For the life of her, Tarra could not fathom why Billy wanted to take her down this road. It pretty well led nowhere or at least it took the long way around to where they were originally headed. Why add miles to the journey?

And then she saw the high gated fence in front of what used to be called Haydock's Farm. Ah, she thought, he wants to see this man, Nate Roden.

But the front gate was high. At least twenty feet high. The whole fence ran across the front entrance at something like a hundred feet and the middle section – where the actual gate opened wide – rose above the main line of fencing to form an arc.

Billy walked across the fenced off area and tried to find a way of looking into its interior grounds. There was a post-box but it opened up so the mail could fall down into a container. You couldn't actually peer through to see what was on the other side. Billy became agitated and wondered how he could gain access. For sure, he couldn't shin up the fence – too high, too sheer.

The entrance had been expanded by some margin. Tarra remembered when Haydock's barn stood here, the entrance was a single wooden gate and rows of barbed wire. The barn itself was old, made by hand by Haydock and his Sons out of all available pieces of timber they could lay their dishonest hands upon for the notion of paying for materials and professional wood-merchants to do the job would revile a miser like old man Haydock. The resulting construction looked like it had maybe three weeks of life left in it and that was only if it didn't rain. The fact that the barn withstood all weathers for more than twenty years was a testament to its resolve and possibly the building skills of the Haydock's.

In fact, it was still a standing construction by the time of old man Haydock's death. It was only when this piece of scrubland had been purchased by this outsider, Roden, who had so infuriated William Telling, that the barn was officially razed to the ground and its surrounding nature reserve worked on for nearly eighteen months. No-one who passed by the protective fencing ever saw what was being built and though the neighbours weren't exactly nearby, the locals hoped the new building would at least fit in with the surrounding area as many of the homes had been built from a completely different era.

But with the fencing so high it was impossible to tell what the new construction looked like and the new owner certainly hadn't held any grand 'Opening-day' party to get to know the neighbours when he'd moved in.

Billy was determined to find out at least what this place looked like. Running along the lanes either side of the fence were sturdy trees and he scrambled up the one which was nearest to the new neighbour's home to overlook what was inside the compound.

As he did so, having beckoned to Tarra to keep her protestations quiet, she heard a thumping noise. She'd heard it when they had arrived but hadn't placed it as being so close to where they were standing. In fact, it was coming from within the compound – just yards away from where she was standing. She ventured closer to the large and solidly built front gate fence and placed her ear against it. Yes, the thumping sound definitely came from the other side of this gate. She looked up and saw Billy was now above the fence line and he was staring down into whatever was on that side of the compound. He then shimmied down and pushed his way from the trunk of the tree. The expression on his face was hard to read save to say he wasn't happy. He strode up to her and instead of quietly telling her what he had seen, he physically pushed past her even though there was enough room to drive by her in a car and headed towards the MG which had been parked about a quarter of a mile down the lane. He got into the car when she was still standing there and he gestured – with his hand, not his voice – for her to get in. She caught up with him, got into the car and waited to hear what he had seen but his face was as a dark cloud waiting to burst out with rain. Instead of his usual practice of turning the ignition on and then revving the bloody thing, he just allowed the car to hum its sound and then he quietly reversed it all the way back to the long lane until it reached the entrance. He carefully manoeuvred the car onto the main road and then – and *then* – he gunned the engine and sped away - but by this time, they were at least a quarter of a mile away from where Haydock's old barn used to stand.

His face remained a scowl as he stared at the road ahead.

What the hell had he seen?

C H A P T E R   1 0
BACK-UP

The same evening, following from Billy and Tarra's un-arranged visit to the Roden home, there was in fact, a birthday party laid on for the elder Beddoes daughter, Patrice, who had just turned 21 years of age. After a few years of cold silence and estrangement between the two friends, following Edmund's scandalous behaviour and running away, Tarra had been invited to the party. She was pleased about the invitation as she and Patrice had been genuine friends and their estrangement had hurt Tarra very much. Patrice was a year younger to Tarra and while Tarra loved being in the company of her 12-year old sister, there are only so many things an age-gap sibling relationship can endure. No doubt, Patrice felt the same about her sister, Phillipa. Tarra had had many friends growing up and, in truth, she missed their friendships as well after the Daddy scandal broke and the Browne's suddenly became lepers in the colony. The birthday party would, she hoped, signal the end of the estrangement and they could be pals again.

If her invitation was a welcome surprise, the invitation to Billy to also attend came as a shock. There was no friendship between the Beddoes' and the Telling's families and so Billy being invited was odd to say the least.

As was the invitation to the new neighbour – for Nate Roden was also in attendance. It took Tarra a few moments to understand why Annaliza had invited this new neighbour until she recalled the sports car-versus-the horse incident and the jogging stranger who had rescued Phillipa. Nate Roden.

Halfway through the party, she then learned why Billy had been invited. Mister Gerald Beddoes – not in attendance at the party – and William Telling were semi-regular business associates in the City –

49

exactly what not even Annaliza seemed to know – and out of expedient courtesy for her Husband, Annaliza had invited the vicious Son-of-a… into her Daughter's party. She bit her lip when that particular invitation went out but money is money and Husband Gerald had looked at her in mocking pity when she told him why she didn't want Billy Telling to attend. Annaliza resented her Husband's manner of domineering her will when she had made a perfectly sound argument as to why the junior Telling should not be there but the house they lived in, the horses their Daughter's rode, the cars they all drove in were all results from sound business arrangements which included Telling Senior and sometimes this meant keeping company with some pretty low forms of life. Billy Telling fitted that description quite nicely but his Father did not and that was the reason, he told her, why he must be at the party. She seethed – but wrote the invitation out, dramatically spat at it and sent it out in next morning's post.

What was not on the invitation list were the names of the two men who sauntered in to The Keys pub and made straight for where Billy was standing. Tarra was still angry with his behaviour of the previous week, frightening Phillipa, and had made her feelings known when she clouted him in front of his friends in this very pub. She was a little perplexed as to his off-mood manner when he'd skinned down the tree having taken a good long look over the fence surrounding Roden's home. All the way home he didn't tell what he'd seen over the fence and so the question she asked about the continued thumping went unanswered. As was his usual manner, he drove the MG too fast across lanes never designed for such speed and scowling down the road as if it were an actual impediment to his desires. What she did notice was when either traffic or a person was directly ahead of him, he slowed down until he was past it or it past him – *THAT* was new. Billy generally didn't care for observing the niceties of road ethics even if meant scaring he hell out of other motorists or pedestrians. Today, he was more cautious.

The two men who were definitely *NOT* on Annaliza's invitation list – mainly because they were really not from this area and not members of her society shit-list – were Donnie Robinson and Cliff Boley. Both men were from the Saxmundhem area and, Tarra knew, were trained competitive fighters in the martial arts arenas. While Billy was not exactly up to their standard, Tarra knew he had taken lessons from both men. They were the same age as Billy and had advantages he did not. They were independently wealthy and did not have to rely on the Bank-of-Dad to buy their jewellery or fast cars – and they could attract women with little more than a smile and a wink. Neither were married and their playboy lifestyle was the envy of most of the younger men who were at this party tonight. If a comparison was to be made between them and Billy – it would be along the lines of they were Monte Carlo and he was Blackpool Beach – but they were friends and for some reason they were here tonight.

When Robinson and Boley met Billy, they huddled away in the corner of the pub and the conversation, mostly from Billy, appeared to be quite intense. Tarra tried to fix her brain on exactly what they were all about – for sure this was no casual trip for the two men – all the way here at a pub they wouldn't wash their hands in. No, some mischief was afoot and Billy was the primer.

Aside from that mystery, the party went into the evening in full swing of happiness and japes. Phillipa had come dressed in a Disney Princess costume and was accordingly treated like Royalty by all – genuine affection and love for this girl who was greatly appreciated by all – along with Lainey Browne as both girls enjoyed the local events, horses, theatre, and were respectful to all around.

Towards the shank of the evening – because the younger elements of the party had early start's the following day – the festivities slowed down and the stewards began their night's duties starting with the canopy tent, then to pack up equipment from the DJ's desk, the tables folded, the glassware taken back into The Keys and parents coming to speak with Annaliza to thank her for a wonderful children's night. In a fairly short time, the masses had all but emptied the pub and were making their way home.

It was at this point, Tarra saw exactly what Billy had planned for *his* part of the enjoyment. As the interior of the pub began to fill with older drinkers not attached to the Beddoes party and were now grateful the screams of the pups and kittens were dying down. The Landlord, Ivan Baxter seemed to have something on his mind because his usual joviality as Mein Host was absent this evening and he kept scanning his eyes to where Billy and his two friends were still huddled in the bar.

Tarra had been grateful for one thing: Billy had stayed off the usual amount of booze he could happily sink when he wasn't driving his car - and this night, he hadn't brought the MG. Now he only lived a mile from The Keys but walking long distances, especially at night, was not an activity Billy indulged in and usually he brought his MG to the place if only to spin it around the car park once or twice to get everyone's attention.

But not tonight.

And when Tarra was catching up with Patrice on her latest advancements – quite advanced – she saw how the evening was going to be played out.

The main thrust of the remaining elders who had attended the party were now tucked away on the other side of the pub and in the Snug. This part of the bar contained just a few older farmers, a couple of diners, herself and Patrice – and Billy with his two mates. It was when Nate Roden passed them by to spend a penny that she was alerted to the night's main activity.

Billy watched Nate exit the bar and enter the toilet and he drew that man's action to the attention of Robinson and Boley. They waited for Nate's exit then stood and walked to the centre of the snug which was mostly empty of customers.

Robinson took position by the bar, Boley stood by a window as if he were just casually scanning the activities outside. There was a loud cough – so overly dramatic – by Billy, and Boley turned to watch Nate Roden coming back from the toilet. When he was about to exit the bar, Boley made his pitch.

'Nate,' he called out, as if they were actual friends.

Tarra broke away from Patrice who had now been joined by another former friend of hers whose company had also been largely invisible in the past few years – but then she did work for her own Father in the City and her job involved trips to Europe and the States.

Nate appeared curious by the call – and stared at the man who'd made it. Tarra watched. It was obvious he didn't know Boley but he'd stopped in his tracks and walked to where Boley stood. As he did, Billy leaned back in his chair and smiled. Not a pleasant smile, the smile of a trouble-maker. You bastard, Tarra thought, you've set this man up for a beating – by two experienced martial arts exponents. And as he leaned back, he watched Robinson walk closer to Nate's back.

Tarra was compelled to warn Nate that he'd been set up but curiosity stopped her. This was the first time she had actually had a good look at Nate Roden. Yes, older than they were, by some margin – but there was… *something.*

She couldn't put her finger on what that something was – how could she? She didn't know the man beyond the friendly way he'd spoken to her when he'd guided baby duck up the embankment. But there was something about him which told her – woman's intuition? – that this was a man who was… *experienced…* in matters of an unfriendly nature.

He stood just a few feet away from Boley – all confident martial arts trained Boley. He did not speak, not even to ask how Boley even knew his name. He just stood there and allowed the man who called him to take the next step.

And Boley did exactly that.

'You have upset the locals around here, Nate – some of whom are friends of mine. You been making threats against a mate.'

Nate did not respond with a verbal protest as most people would. No denials, no questions as to who he'd upset, no kind of reaction at all actually. He watched his adversary smile, just a few seconds worth as if the man was expecting some kind of denying retort. When the man Boley was trying to intimidate did not appear intimidated, the confident smile wavered – *just a smidgen* – but enough to give Nate Roden an idea of his opponent's worth. This hesitation was followed then by a small step towards Nate Roden and an eyeful glare intended to do more than just intimidate – it was intended to frighten the proposed victim. Boley narrowed his eyes and adopted a near smiling rictus grin. 'You need to watch your step - *Rodent…*' he threatened and stretched out his left hand.

There was no denying Boley's physical strength. He was tall, taller than Nate, and, clearly, he was trained, for even under the summer jacket, Nate could see a bulging upper arm. The push then, Boley's left hand up against Nate's right chest was hard enough to knock Nate off-balance and stepping backwards.

When this physical confrontation happened, Tarra wondered if she had mis-read Nate Roden for the expression on his face was one of fear and surprise. She wondered if he was not the formidable man she had imagined him to be – based on… what? His gentlemanly gesture when she was riding the horse, his act of showing kindness at assisting a helpless duckling, his rescuing of young Phillipa Beddoes when Billy sped through the village street.

His next act dis-spelled the notion immediately.

As Nate stepped backwards, Donnie Robinson stepped from the bar with his right hand aimed at Nate's right shoulder. The intention being – and he and Cliff Boley had exercised this stunt before – to grab the victim by the shoulder, drag him slightly back, suddenly place both hands underneath the victim's armpits, bring the hands up, clasp them together behind the victim's head to perform a Half-Nelson. This would then be followed by Boley striking said victim in the solar plexus with one, very nasty blow. It would be enough to render any average man to a blubbering mess on the floor, trying to get his breath back, in pain, eyes watering, in no way able to respond to such a devastating blow. It had been used many times to great effect by the two trained fighters.

But not this time.

As Nate stepped back and felt his jacket being man-handled by the unseen adversary. He stamped down, hard, on the man's instep and as Robinson yelled out in pain, Nate followed it up by striking him in the groin with the side of his open hand. The grunt of pain from the foot stamping was replaced by a shrill shriek but even this didn't last longer than a second as Nate brought up a clenched fist and struck Robinson with the back of his hand – a direct hit on the man's nose. Robinson was propelled backwards, fell against the bar counter and collapsed to the floor, spark out.

This act apparently had a number of different reactions. Behind the bar, Ivan Baxter had been standing by one of the sinks when he saw what happened to the young well-educated and prosperous friend of his regular customer, Billy Telling. Billy had already passed his £20 to Baxter to look the other way should any physical altercation occur and Ivan was happy to provide his regular customers with a favour…

But this arrangement didn't include the supposed victim from retaliating – *in his bar for God's sake* – and dropping one of the intimidators. He cast a nervous glance to the hitherto smiling Billy – who now was not smiling – and moved to the front of the bar where he was joined by three elders of the village who were not in the least bit upset about what had just happened.

Now, Cliff Boley had prepared for his next action – and was therefore surprised when his thug-at-arms comrade suddenly took a dive and was apparently out of this world in an unconscious stupor. This resulted in Boley hesitating before he delivered what should have been the finishing strike – and the hesitation was long enough for Nate Roden to make his strike.

It was perfectly delivered straight blow to Boley's face – just left of the mouth, a tad under the lower lip and slightly above the chin. As the punch was delivered, Nate grabbed Boley's jacket collar and snarled – 'The name is Roden…' and Boley dropped to the floor – not quite unconscious but definitely no longer in the game.

Which left a terrified Billy Telling to ponder what was going to happen to him. The smug smile Tarra had seen on his face turned to a mouth wide opened and the look of terror in his eyes.

Ivan Baxter found his pub proprietor's voice.

'Oi,' he shouted, 'I'll 'ave no violence in 'ere.' To which a protesting voice shouted back 'Shurrup, Baxter – first bit of excitement we 'ad in the bloody place since you took over.' Ivan Baxter felt his status as pub proprietor being ridiculed and slunk back behind the bar, out of sight.

Nate Roden then turned his full attention to Billy Telling. From the little Tarra had witnessed, there was no way Nate could have realised these two poncified thugs were actually working in tandem with Billy and so she couldn't understand how Nate had correctly worked out that they were.

No words, no threats, nothing came from Nate as he squared up to Billy, suddenly grabbing him by the throat. The thumb dug into Billy's Adam's Apple and the remaining fingers positioned at the side of his neck. Billy was pushed back against the wall. Tarra watched as he slowly elevated by a good few inches and she realised Nate was physically lifting him off the floor – *by his throat*. She looked down at Billy's feet and saw he was standing on tiptoe.

Billy was turning a dark purple so clearly, he was in pain as well as being terrified and humiliated in front of just twelve people – but one of the people was Tarra and her look of horror at what was happening to him was painful to watch.

He made to lessen Nate's grip by placing both of his hands around Nate's arms. This was met by an angry snarl. 'Touch my arms, Telling, and I'll choke you to death.' In Billy's terrified state, he formed the opinion that Roden's threat was genuine and dropped his hands away.

It was Tarra who saved Billy – and the day – from this man who had not appeared as a threat before but now was positively frightening.

'Please, Mister Roden,' she begged, 'he's an asshole who thinks he's got power and brains. If you hurt him, it will mean Police and you could get into trouble and he's really not worth it.' For good measure, she then added, 'And think how it would spoil Patrice's party if we get the bloody Cops crashing in here.'

Her wise words and frightened voice were just enough to soothe the savage soul which clearly lay deep inside Nate Roden's person and after a few seconds, he released his grip around Billy's throat. The pathetic little trouble-maker slid to the floor, coughing and spluttering, and brought his knees up to his head, hands clutching at them tightly. Nate did not even look at Tarra as he turned away and strode away – but he made a small glance in Ivan Baxter's direction as he exited the pub. When this bloody nonsense is over and done with, Baxter told himself, I'll be wanting more than £20 from young Telling.

The excitement lasted a few minutes longer as some of the customers popped in from other areas of the pub to see what had just taken place. They saw two seemingly unconscious men and a blubbering wreck who looked as though he'd been involved in a full-scale war. In the middle of this part of the room, a young woman was staring at the blubbering wreck and they wondered if she was the paramour to the blubbering wreck.

The landlord stormed around to the room and demanded the blubbering wreck get off the bloody floor, pick up his bloody mates, cough up the promised dosh and then get himself and his two unconscious mates the hell out of the pub or he will be calling the Cops himself. He also stared at Tarra – a girl he knew but only barely – and saw the scorn on her face. She knew.

Tarra stood over Billy with the new expression of disgust. She knew he had brought those posh knobs from Saxmundhem to this party with the express purpose of harming one of his host's guests. Apparently, the landlord was also involved as he had mentioned "promised dosh" – which meant a bribe to look the other way if a fight suddenly broke out. It wouldn't mean anything to Billy if the fight had turned nasty and if it had resulted in broken furniture – just so long as it also resulted in a broken Nate Roden. He would happily pay for the broken chairs and table.

On the table where Billy and the two would-be hard boys had been sitting, there were two tall glasses of Lager. She picked up both and poured them over the still heavy breathing Billy and this insult was ended with her seething expression and comment – *'You prize plum'* - to Billy Telling. She left him where he lay in his own mess and went outside to check on Nate.

After a ten-minute search of trying to find Nate, she found her Mummy, Lainey, Annaliza and Patrice instead. She didn't mention the unpleasantness which had just taken place inside the pub and they were still happily saying their 'Good night's' to lingering guests so clearly they hadn't been made aware of the incident. Annaliza told Tarra, before she'd had the chance to ask if they'd seen Mister Roden, that the nice Mister Roden had just bought Phillipa a year's free riding at the Tierney Farm as a birthday present and Phillipa was thrilled. 'Wasn't that sweet of him?' said Annaliza. 'And we barely know him.' As innocently as she could, Tarra asked if they'd seen him and they told her he had to leave the party early as he had an early start tomorrow morning – a job in the City to tackle – and they went away leaving Tarra out of joint and frustrated. Her boyfriend – about to become an *EX* – was still on the floor and looking like the biggest stuffed turkey seen since Christmas and the man she was finding to be more enigmatic than she had previously considered was now on his way home. And no chance of seeing him tomorrow from the sound of things.

Tomorrow, she decided, she would go to Haydock's farm and leave him a letter of apology, stating she had not known beforehand what Billy was intending and hoping he was alright after this unprovoked attack and hadn't been hurt.

As she pondered this plan, wondering at the same time why she would even care for this near total stranger, she was brought back to Earth by the sound of two men dragging one unconscious man out of the pub and another two men – Billy and Boley – assisting each other out. Billy spied her staring at him and as he opened his hands in a "Forgive-me" gesture, Tarra walked away and joined her Mum and Sister.

C H A P T E R   1 1

BASHKIM'S SHAME

Devishi Bartok stood on the balcony in the rain and stared out across the hilly plain which surrounded Vanna Bashkim's little Kingdom. He hid his temper from what he had just witnessed inside the Bashkim home. The rain wasn't bothering him – but watching Vanna Bashkim sobbing into his hands had and he could stomach no more.

Inside the large lounge, which could potentially hold more than fifty people plus many tables of food and drink should Bashkim ever feel the desire to have a party, he, Marku Kursk, Oska Gorovitch and Zebo Tulse sat in silence.

Like Bartok, Kursk and Gorovitch sat in embarrassed silence as their host and fellow member of the Albanian Shqiptose heaved his tears into his hands one moment then wiping the slime and snot away from his hands with a large soiled handkerchief in another. He had been crying for some time now and the disgust felt by his fellow comrades in arms was demonstrably palpable. At least, from Kursk and Gorovitch.

Only Zebo Tulse showed no emotion, or disgust at the disgraceful way his former friend was behaving now. He knew emotional outbursts sometimes dictated a man's actions towards uncontrollable despair – even in men such as they. He had suffered the loss of a Son under curious and tragic circumstances and now it appeared Vanna Bashkim had experienced the same loss – and possibly by the same hand. Unlike Vanna however, Zebo had kept his grief under control and he would never dare demonstrate publicly such an outburst such as the one he was witnessing now. He had shown Vanna the filmed footage on the Mnsk boy's phone and when he saw how Tito had died, Vanna broke down. Grief for a Father from a Father who had suffered the same loss.

59

The image was frozen at the same point Zebo had made at his own home – the clearest image of the face of the man who had slain his Son. He expected some kind of shock from Vanna – that was to be expected – but this outpouring of groaning and sobbing was too much and underneath the tableau of emotion, Zebo felt something was wrong.

He stood and, unbidden, walked to the table where bottles of wines were stacked and he poured himself a glass. He did not pour anything for his colleagues nor for Vanna. He pulled a chair on wheels away from a work-desk and took it to sit next to Vanna, sitting on his huge sofa.

He kept his voice level and calm – but this was business and he needed Vanna to register the reason why he and his comrades were here. He took the man's once muscular arm and pried it away from his reddened face which was now awash with tears.

Many years ago, Vanna Bashkim had been a wrestler-cum-strongman in a Circus and in his prime, he was man to view with fear. Six feet ten inches in height, ninety-five kg in weight and most of it was muscle, he was the most formidable character around the southern areas of Albania. It was only ever a matter of time before his fighting skills would be employed by the men who ruled the townships and city establishments such as the nightclubs which were opening up along the lines of the streets of Las Vegas. His power brought him wealth and a steady rise in the ranks of those powerful men until his own Patrone gave him a living and Family he could lead as he got older where fighting was now the domain of the younger foot-soldiers. To remember him from those days and now to see him thus was a shock to those who had grown up with him and had watched in awe as he ploughed his way through all oppositions to establish his own identity as a member of the Shqiptose.

It was an incident, just a few years earlier, which began the destabilization of Vanna Bashkim. He had many vanities in his life – as most men in power are prone to – and one of them was the accumulation of wealth. Any venture which would involve the building of his own power-base and increase his status in financial matters was to be entertained and one of Bashkim's vanities was his undoubted talent in cards games. Nearly every game in cardplaying was known to him and, in truth, he was an exponent in most of them, winning more than he ever lost.

Until…

Until one very large game in Skopia three years ago in one of its largest hotels and a game which eventually went down in local history for it lasted four days with the players getting very little rest – no doubt having an unsettling effect on those who lasted from Game 1 to the competition's final Game. Ten men started and only two sat in the final Game. Bashkim was one of the two.

The upshot was that he lost the winning pot of £10,000,000. The loss disgraced him and much of his credibility as a Leader of the kind of Family he was known for began to sink. His respect from so many dwindled as did his stature. Those who were considered his equals and Bartok, Gorovitch and Kursk were included in that number, saw him as a weakened man. Zebo had even publicly condemned him as being a foolish man who had weakened his stature and from that point, Vanna Bashkim was looked at askance by those powerful men – and by those who climbed the ladder of violence below him.

Now, in his early seventies, his once huge frame had seemingly shrunk. The arms of muscular power seemed barely able to carry an average bag of shopping. His weight was diminished and he was no longer a man of power. Perhaps this explained his weakness here in his home and the pathetic display of overwhelming emotion in the presence of his former friends and comrades.

'Do you recognise this man, Vanna?' asked Zebo, gently, not angry, don't force him, guide him until another's friendly voice would help end the tears pouring from his eyes. He would then know he was in the company of comrades and their empathy and compassion would surround him until he could function again – as a man. Zebo asked the same question and now Kursk and Gorovitch had edged closer to the sofa in order to hear the man speak. Bartok re-entered the room from the balcony and joined his comrades.

It took Vanna some time to stare at the freeze frame and understand he was looking at the face of Tito's killer.

And then, the horrible truth came pouring from his mouth. Edon, his bastard offspring, the Son who, once upon a time, would possibly have been destined to take over Vanna's mantle as Patrone of the Bashkim Family, had become the very Devil Incarnate, he wailed in front of his comrades. His Son's temper and sense of judgement – both necessary attributes to be kept under proper check in such an elevated position – were constantly erratic and, on too many occasions, ran flat out of control. On too many occasions Edon had openly challenged his Father's authority in front of the other Soldiers and in their eyes Vanna, as a man, had diminished in consequence. In one very angry instant, the furious Edon had actually physically lashed out, not only striking at Vanna but at his half siblings and the Bashkim Advisor, Milo Tarn. Such behaviour had to be dealt with and when Edon was taken aside by Tarn who advised him to control his outrages, Edon not only lashed out at the unfortunate Advisor but then flew into an uncontrollable fury and left the home for four days during which period of time he vented his anger and wrath out on innocent members of the Bashkim community, resulting in hospital and Police activity.

It was then Vanna Bashkim made his decision to eradicate Edon from the Family altogether. He said so now, out loud, and now Zebo, Bartok, Kursk and Gorovitch were all rapt attention. Naturally, Vanna could not kill his own Son – anybody else's, yes, and with ease, but his own flesh and blood…?

Through foreign contacts, he explained, Tarn was put in touch with an Intermediary-Agent who could introduce him to a man who could either take Edon to task – or take Edon out of the frame completely. Tarn took this latter option to Vanna and advised him accordingly. Edon's fury came from a place deep within his psyche and was not subject to the conformities laid out by the Bashkim Regime. It took Vanna less than ten minutes to make his decision and this was passed onto the Agent by Tarn.

Edon Bashkim, bastard Son of Patrone Vanna Bashkim, would have to be removed from the Family Unit completely.

Once the instruction was given, the Agent took his leave. The two primary points of the deal would be the deed itself and the subsequent payment upon the Service delivered to the satisfaction of the Employer. Tarn did not need to enquire any further – it was a given there would be no mistakes or further communications between the hiring faction or the person tasked to do the job and no questions would be asked about method.

And the method was so simple: A stranger creating a distraction and an assassin taking Edon's life in that distracted moment.

And as everyone in the room now knew, the task was successful. The only extra consequence, not to anyone's satisfaction, was the subsequent slaying of Tito Tulse just a couple of days later. Were the two deaths of two Sons a coincidence or was Edon's assassin the same man he was looking at on Zebo's mobile phone? If so, how did that come about? Why was the assassin even still in Albania so long after the job on Edon been executed?

Question: Had immediate payment to the Agent been made? Here, Tarn, who had previously secreted himself away from the group came out from his own Office and answered that question.

Yes, he confirmed. Payment had been made the same day. It was the agreed amount and the Agent was satisfied. The communication ended and no further communication could be made again.

Question: Was the man who had created the distraction the same man on Zebo's phone. For this, the only man with Edon that day who actually was close enough to see the stranger was sent for.

Edon's bodyguard, Davidoff, arrived and visibly demonstrated his resentment for the fact that he was being interrogated by Zebo Tulse – a man he hated for his slow continued eradication of Vanna Bashkim's authority as a Patrone in the Shqiptose Cartel.

Vanna had, by now, regained control of his grieving - and he stood aside as Zebo showed the image to his Son's bodyguard. But Davidoff shrugged his shoulders and said this man, Tito's killer, was nothing like the man who had confronted Edon and his entourage seconds before he was assassinated. And when the shooting furore was over, when Davidoff and his companions had cautiously come out of hiding to take their chances, when they saw their Leader lying on the ground, blood and viscera everywhere, the sight of his nearly obliterated head almost ripped away from his shoulders, it took a few minutes before they even registered the disappearance of the man who had halted their promenade – in order to have them standing still while the sniper assassin took aim at… Edon? – and there was no further sign of him as they scoured the area.

Conclusions then. Possibly the assassin who took Edon Bashkim's life could also be the man who had killed Tito – if that was the case, he was working in tandem with another – the man who had halted the group while he used the rifle to slay Edon. A concerted action – a concerted DOUBLE action even – for if the two deaths were connected by the same killer it may suggest there could be more deaths to follow. More deaths – of Sons of the Fathers who had waged their own wars against the establishments for decades, successfully neutering the legal Laws of the land, turning Albania into a lawless community, spreading its criminal tentacles to other countries, the slave trade, prostitution, extortion, murder. Perhaps these two deaths were the beginning of a policy of retribution, local, national or even international, legal or maybe even another kind of violence entering Albanian society from another faction – getting rid of the old guard by killing off the young pretenders destined to take their places following the demise of their Fathers. Zebo knew he had only a short time left to maintain his current status before his own offspring would assume his mantle and he could then retire into old age, grow tomatoes and make wine, live out his remaining years in peace while the youngest of their tribes showed their mettle in defying the Government and the Church and the Law.

This interview with the diminished Vanna had yielded nothing positively conclusive except for only one tiny clue, issued by Tarn. He was of the opinion that the Agent was not from this side of the globe. Tarn, who eloquently spoke a number of languages, had conversed with the Intermediary-Agent in English.

This was interesting to Zebo. A European connection – well, it would make sense. Only a blind fool would hire such a person to commit such a deed from his own doorstep. Yes, the assassin would have be from outside the Albanian borders. And English. This was not to say the assassin was from the United Kingdom but it was a start.

Zebo requested the method of how to contact the Agent – with a view to repeat the exercise of how the assassin was brought in. Tarn, eager for this interview to come to a speedy and easy end, furnished Zebo with the Intermediary-Agent's name and geographical whereabouts. As it turned out, an area within two plane trips from Albania – a mission Tanka could carry out without too much trouble and this would happen at the soonest interval.

This interview with Vanna Bashkim came to an end and the visitors left the old man to grieve for the death of his Son – the death he had arranged. How his conscience would tolerate that act only time would tell but the sight of the once powerful Vanna Bashkim sobbing his grief out in the company of his comrades had disturbed them and they left him with the taste of disgust in their mouths.

C H A P T E R 1 2
TARRA'S FANTASY LAND

It took Tarra two days to compose the letter of apology which she hoped would explain and at least separate her from Billy's actions against Mister Roden. She didn't know why but she wanted to keep in with his company – she didn't address the question, even to herself, as to why as she barely knew him. He was at least 20 years older than she and he was a kind of man very different to those she was more familiar with in her home area. It was how he had dealt with Boley and Robinson which was uppermost in her mind as she had attempted to compose letters of apology – five in total. The fifth was at least coherent and didn't drag on about her relationship with Billy – which she had now determined would come to an end. She had grown and he hadn't. His immaturity was accepted in their school days but not now. And what he had attempted to do to Mister Roden in The Keys went beyond the pale.

She approached Haydock's Barn – she still thought of it in that particular term – and was now extremely tentative. In truth, she did not owe him any kind of apology, or even explanation, for Billy's actions in hiring the two thugs to work him over but she had written one anyway – perhaps to ingratiate herself with him in at least a friendly way.

A hundred yards away from the front gates, she heard the same thumping sounds she and Billy had heard two days ago. Perhaps he was chopping wood for the forthcoming winter – did he have a coal and wood fire and not radiators? The thumping sound was too regular and constant and too long lasting for him to be chopping wood. There would have been pauses in between the chop action and the picking up of the chopped wood. She even contemplated sneaking up the same tree Billy had climbed to get a look at the new area – she wondered how different it would look. Back then – the last time she'd been able to see it – the barn was surrounded by at least a dozen or so trees – one of which had actually grown *inside* the barn – Haydock having built his construction around the plant life without removing any of it. A small tree had grown so large and tall it protruded out of the roof of the barn which stood at least thirty feet tall. What of that area was left now that it had become the living domain of a human?

She got her answer quickly and without the need to climb the tree for the main gates, central to the tall wooden fence which surrounded the area, were both open. Again, tentatively, she slowed her walk and peered into the area beyond the gates as the thumping was now more immediate to where she was standing.

What she saw took her breath away.

Only eight trees in their original state still stood, untouched. Four trees had been carved into ornate totem-styled statues, standing at least eighteen feet tall, and were set around a large compound of delightful sights. The other four trees had been reconstructed in a manner suited for climbing, not only up but also across for there were rope ladders and rope pathways connecting each tree to the others.

At the far end of the compound, set below the surrounding fence, she could see colourful bushes of flowers and three beehives. Mister Roden had provided an environment and home for bees to come and do their wonderous act of making honey. She wondered if he was an apiarist – a bee-keeper who looked after the welfare of those little industrious humming creatures who in turn made a food to be consumed. She knew a man who did exactly that who lived only a mile away from this place and wondered if Mister Roden and Mister Edgeley were friends who worked together for the benefit of bees.

As well as glorious flowerings, she saw a man-made water fountain where a small waterfall poured into three shell-like canopies. Even from this distance she could see all three canopies were occupied with feathered birds enjoying either a drink or playing splash in the small baths.

A short distance away from all things natural or man-made, she saw a large table where at least six blackbirds were perching and eating food placed on the table.

On the trees, hung nets of bird foods like nuts and seeds and each of the nets – and there must have been close to a dozen – were gainfully attended by all different species of birds. Bees and birds together in an environment where they were safe and felt no fear from the species who had put fear into their lives.

It was a fantasy island for Tarra.

But it was the large house which dominated the scene. Where the barn had once stood – now completely gone – stood a house which reminded her of something she had seen in a film. The film she had found boring – a sword and fantasy drama where constant battles were fought by wizards and small people against monsters and talking trees – but the accommodation belonging to one of the small people had fascinated her and its resemblance was now standing in front of her just twenty yards away.

It was a white building, not made of separated bricks cemented together but of stone all the way around. Seemingly a single level abode with a thatched roof. Very olde worlde she thought, except for the few solar panels which she could see placed on the strawed roofing.

It was all rounds, or what she could see, no straight edges or sharp corners. The windows were huge and were round and were protected by a porch-like effect which was a part of the wall. The door was immense and round – and heavy – also protected by a porch as a part of the wall and not as a fixture added to it. The walls of the house did not come straight down to but veered outwards to join the ground. The whole compound was floored with chippings, tiny chippings, not earth or wholly concrete. The house was directly situated in front of her so she could not see all the way around it but just this glimpse had generated such an interest in her and so she ventured actually fully into the compound.

For Tarra, a lover of nature and of the beasts and the various other creatures of the planet, it was a beautiful man-made fantasy land. She ventured forth to gain a better view.

And now she saw the same thing Billy must have seen when he had climbed the tree and looked down – and it explained the reason why he had chosen to employ the services of Boley and Robinson.

The constant thumping was coming from Mister Roden who was dressed in a tracksuit and was pummelling the hell out of a rubber mannequin which was buried in the ground to keep it positioned in one place. It was the kind of mannequin rugby players would tackle in training. It was made of solid rubber-like substance and did not give much in the way of wavering with each blow so it must have felt very like hitting a real person, bigger and stronger than the attacker, and not like a swinging punchbag where the fighter would have to wait for the swing to come back his way. Mister Roden was standing in one single place and he was swapping his punching with each hand as he laid into the damn thing.

Tarra thought: if he hit any flesh and blood creature that way, as likely as not, he'd kill them. It was that thought which now explained her reason for staying here. She thought about posting the letter she'd written into the post-box which was situated on one of the gate doors when the thumping suddenly stopped and she watched Mister Roden move away to a number of green plastic barrels hidden by the four remaining trees. What purpose the barrels were for she couldn't guess – until he took the lid off one, removed his tracksuit to reveal a near naked body save by just a pair of biking shorts and he picked up a bucket which he plunged into the barrel which contained cold water. He then poured the cold water all over him – three, four times, until he was absolutely soaked all the way through. He picked up a carton and poured liquid soap into his hands and he rubbed it all over his body, thoroughly soaking it in a green lather. Then he repeated the water bucket exercise, continuing to drench himself until all the soap was washed away. He stood still, leaning against one of the barrels as though too exhausted to move. And for all Tarra knew, he may well have been for she had no idea how long he'd been pummelling that poor mannequin. He turned around.

Which was when she saw his body, unclothed save for the shorts, properly for the first time.

Dear God, she thought: is he ripped or what?

His arms were heavily muscled, now because he had just finished a clearly invigorating punching exercise, but his shoulders were broad and his stomach was what her friends were pleased to call a *"full six-pack"*. Clearly, running and cycling were very much a part of his exercise regime for his legs were as powerful looking as his arms.

There wasn't an ounce of wasted flesh on his muscled and tanned body and Tarra was now aware her breathing was laboured and out of control. In all her life, she had only ever seen bodies like this in photographs of celebrities or sportsmen who had dedicated their lives to the love of the perfect human body.

And then he saw her. He picked up a towel and walked towards her. He stopped and stood about twenty yards away from her and she wondered how she could explain this intrusion away without sounding like a dribbling idiot intruder. He scrutinised her for a few moments and Tarra was now wishing she'd sent the bloody letter by post instead. Then he smiled.

'Hullo,' he said.

C H A P T E R   1 3
HOME SWEET FORTESS

Tarra was agog at what she was looking at when she and Nate entered the house. He had already given her a close-up angle of all the sights she had seen when she was still at the front entrance gate but now she was marvelling at the shenanigans of the birds, of so many species, as they enjoyed the gifts laid out for them by this most accommodating human. Birds in the man-made troughs swimming about and flying their wings to dry without actually taking off. The larger birds walking on the wooden table which she could see had been liberally sprinkled with bird seed and small bread crumbs. Birds flying around the trees encircling the hanging bean bags and water containers. Bees buzzing around the many kinds of flowering and then occupying space inside the three hives. Within this single garden, a wonderful paradise had been created for the birds and bees – and possibly other creatures as well for foxes had been known to enter the gardens of the many abodes where once it had been exclusively a fox, bird, badger, deer habitat. Human encroachment had diminished their homes and they wandered where they could. Here in this place it was clear they had consent by its current resident to come and go as they pleased – which pleased Tarra no end as nature was a strong instinct within her.

Having been given the exterior tour, Mister Roden then asked if she would like a drink inside the house and she wobbled slightly before nodding – hiding her eager enthusiasm by some margin.

She had already seen much of the house exterior on the nature walk. It was an odd construction and it took some while for her to realise there were no straight up and down lines. The base of the house was… let's see… as a tree, she described to herself. Its base seemed to grow out of the ground as a tree trunk does – underneath the ground level the

71

tree has its roots working furiously to help its upper half grow up and outwards. The house seemed to do the same thing. The walls were not 90 degrees from the ground to the top but designed slightly inwards, leaning as it were. She saw two more large round windows and another large round rear door on the far side of the house which could not be seen from the entrance gate and one the other side of the rear door there was an equally large window – again round – which contained what room she could only guess at.

She also noticed the house itself was almost completely round – only a topographical picture could confirm that conjecture but it looked as near a perfect round as she could make out from walking around it.

Already transfixed by the house and its thatched roof, she was taken inside via the door she had seen upon first sight of the house. It was clearly built as a defence entry for it was heavy for him to open and then close. There were three separate locks on the inside – and they were solid looking as well. If the door could be viewed as a clock, the top lock was positioned at one o'clock, the second at three o'clock and the third at twenty-five past the clock. Once those locks had been slid across, it would take a battering ram to break this door down.

Security much?

The moment she entered this part of the house, she took a breath for its interior was as captivating as the exterior.

The reception room was huge. It also stood as the breakfast/lunch/dining room and if Mister Roden was inclined to throw a party now and then, this would be where the guests would mostly congregate. Immediately as she entered, she saw it was mostly a carpeted room, a beautiful lush thick off-white carpet which covered practically the whole room apart from the entrance area which was wooden. This area covered a space of around twelve feet by eight feet. Mister Roden gently explained this was where his guests (?) would remove their outdoors footwear and either pad about barefooted or in their socks or change into a variety of soft slippers placed at the side of the entrance. This way, he explained, his carpet would remain clean and his guests could feel at home…

At home? What kind of home has this kind of protection defences?

In the centre of the room was a large table which could seat up to twelve people easily and Tarra wondered then if Mister Roden had a large family which hadn't been seen yet or were on their way from wherever he came from. She didn't enquire.

To her immediate right was the kitchen. Small and compact and separated from the main room for it was situated inside an alcove. It contained a large freezer-fridge, store cabinets at ground and head level, an oven, a washing machine, space for the trash container and then the sink which had two sinks and draining areas. A small round window gave the kitchen a flowing airstream if it was in active use.

The kitchen was contained within an archway and archways pervaded the room. Next to the kitchen was a smaller alcove which was the larder. Next to that another alcove containing cleaning materials and instruments. The alcove was covered by a blue curtain.

'No doors,' she observed. 'Don't like doors,' he replied.

Moving along the wall there was a small alley. At the far end of the alley another alcove which was contained by a sliding panel and the symbolic signs of male and female above it clearly describing the toilet area. There was another room and this was also contained by a sliding panel but unlike the other rooms, this had a control box which resembled a phone dial. She did not enquire about this either and he did not offer an explanation. Perhaps it was too early in this new friendship to explain what a 'Panic-Room' was.

Directly ahead of her was another alley and he walked through it, she behind him. More archways, more blue curtains and he swept one curtain away to show her a bedroom. Large, wardrobed, carpeted, large round window for greeting in the new day. The bed was a double and again Tarra wondered if there was another person in this man's world whom she hadn't seen yet. The alley was long with two more bedrooms, both smaller than the main one, and though there were beds inside the rooms, neither had been set up and the wardrobes were empty of clothing items.

Outside each bedroom, there was a bell-button. He explained. No knocking the doors in this house, if you wanted to enter an occupied bedroom, you pressed the bell chime – which he demonstrated to her, a pleasing sound, designed to capture the resident's attention and not make them jump out of their skin like a Big Ben *DONG* effect. A sweet way to alert someone if you are bringing them a supper or a breakfast

At the end of this alley was another archway also with a sliding panel to close it off to the rest of the general household and they went through it to reveal the house bathroom.

In one part of the room a large round bath dominated – which also contained a jacuzzi. At least five people of average size could easily occupy this design.

Next to it, a shower area – again, a design of size large enough to hold a few people. Clearly, Mister Roden liked space where he walked. No banging his arms or legs in any confined areas in this house.

Here in this room she saw the large round window – or door -she had seen when she was walking outside. There were also three easy chairs perched by the outside wall. Once the bather/s had completed their ablutions, the large window could be opened and they could seat themselves near the now open window and dry off without touching a bath towel.

Her eyes were as wide as round saucers. He took her back where they came from and back into the dining room. From here, there was a wall which separated this room from another, cut off by another blue curtain. He pulled the cord and it swept across and she saw another archway - and the lounge room. They went inside.

Mister Roden liked his comfort. The lounge room was large and partitioned. Where they stood now was where the resident would rest after a hard day's… whatever industry Mister Roden was involved in. In this room was a long leather sofa, again intended for a group of people to use, a large TV set, cupboards, a record player – Tarra had never seen one this tall off the floor – and stacks of vinyl LP's to play on this machine.

No wood or coal fire – just a single radiator. She doubted it would be used much beyond a real hard winter. He took her around the wall partition and here she saw a room designed to be used as a workroom and rest area. A whole computer set-up and smaller equipment used for exercising. She guessed Mister Roden worked here, using the computer to write… whatever his business was – and then, to recover from a sedentary position after hours of gazing at a computer, he would exercise for about ten minutes to liberate his body from the long sitting down. She wondered what his business was. Whatever it was it must be lucrative. Taking the Aston Martin and now this whole house into consideration, this man must be at least a millionaire three or four times over.

He instructed her to make use of the kitchen area while he put on some light clothing. She had poured two cups of tea when he returned now wearing jogging bottoms and a sports vest. They sat at the window where two comfy leather chairs and a small round table was positioned. From here, through the round window, they could view much of the garden. She saw his exercise area and how much of it was incorporated into the standing trees.

'Do you like my home?' he asked.

She tried not to gush and failed the moment she opened her mouth. It is the most beautiful home she had ever seen she told him. Everything was… fantasia style. She questioned him about the fact that there were no straight lines, no sharp corners, no doors to open outwards. He answered quite simply – he did not like confinements and he thought angular elements like rectangles and squares were aesthetically ugly. Round things were much more pleasing to the eye, he told her. She stared at him. He was smiling as he spoke and her eyes were glazed. He had an accent – not foreign but not English – certainly not a local to the Suffolk area – but he did not tell her where he came from. He told her he was a writer – hence the computer set-up - but not what he wrote for a living. As he spoke, she was sensing a relaxing sensation for his voice was almost hypnotic. She could listen to this voice read the menu at Gianni's Restaurant in Lowestoft where she and her family went to dine once every month and it would still sound like he was reading a love story between two cursed lovers who were fighting to shout their love to their feuding families before finally reaching their happy ever after moment.

Tarra did not believe – or never had done up till now – in love at first sight but now she was sizing Mister Roden up. Her first sight of him being so proper when he had seen her and her group on horseback, when the two Police cars could have possibly have turned the happy riding day into something more tragic. His kind assistance to the duckling, his rescue of Phillipa Beddoes when Billy-boy had played silly-sods in his MG Sports car and then a few nights back when he dealt with the two pillocks brought in by Billy to inflict punishment for his threat to Telling Senior following the Beddoes/horse incident.

All these things – and now a home fit for even a member of Royalty to sail through and be impressed - and Tarra was aware she was gazing – not looking or staring – but gazing at Mister Roden. This resulted in a self-defence posture. Tarra had always been the person in control of the attractions-between-the-sexes and up to this point, that arrangement was fairly easy for she had only ever known males of her own age and class. Most of them were thundering bores but they served a current purpose if she wanted to go to a place and not use public service transport, or dinner on a Sunday at University when the refectory was closed and she was stony-broke. Her beauty – her vivacious personality and demeanour – had captivated nearly all the boys/men she had ever come into contact with. Even Daddy's now notorious escapades with money not his and a girl half his age had not left her completely isolated. The best of the not very good bets was Billy Telling and up to now she had been relatively happy with that arrangement. In truth, even before recent days events, she knew Billy was never going to be a long-term situation but he filled a gap.

This gap however, was going to prove something not equal to Billy-boy's limited charms or character. Compared to Mister Roden, Billy Telling was smaller than small-fry, not even in the same room as a person who could converse on a dozen subjects and still be interesting without being condescending and on the lowest rung of the social ladder when it came to a physical description.

For the first time in her life – well, certainly in the past six years – Tarra was confounded by a lack of ability to converse with a man. She was not Mister Roden's equal, she knew, but then she didn't even know what Mister Roden's status was. That was confusing. I'm not as good as he is, she told herself – but I don't even know what level his '*GOOD*' is. Bereft of something worthy to say, she opted for silence…

…until she saw the two designs on his forearms.

Now, when Tarra was in University, many of her friends had decided to have tattoos put on their bodies. Any tattoo, any design, as long as it was visible when they were on the beach, in the skimpiest of bikinis. All her friends were loud and visible in personality and, accordingly, all had opted for tattoos of one ostentatious design or another and had them placed on their arms or legs, or both, covering a sizeable portion of their bodies.

Tarra did not like tattoos at all – she thought they were repulsive. She recalled her Grandfather – a sailor from his RN days and always showing off his tattoo of a girl dancer on his left arm and a portrait of a Japanese Geisha girl he had met when serving in Japan on his right arm. It was fun to show off when he was a younger man but when he'd aged and his arms became weathered and wrinkled, they were less attractive and she told her friends she did want to be tattooed. She relented when one of them showed her a tiny dove design on her ankle. Tarra relented and copied her friend.

Striving for something to say which could at least bring about conversation, she saw two designs on Mister Roden's arms and she said, 'Nice tattoos.'

He smiled and looked at them. They're not tattoos he told her and he straightened his arms out to show her. She had to lean forward, slightly confused, to see what he was demonstrating. It took her a few moments to see exactly what he was showing her.

'Oh my God,' she said.

They weren't tattoos – they were brands.

C H A P T E R 1 4
THE NEPALESE JOURNEY

Tarra sat back and gleaned every word Mister Roden was telling her. At least now he was taking the lead in their converse and what he told her was as fascinating as she could have hoped it would be given the imaginative picture she had conjured up in her head about him and even romantic in a non-romance way.

At the age of 17, he had left his family and home, for which there had never been much love or attachment, far behind to see what else was out there in the big bad world. He first went to University to study a randomly chosen subject and quickly discovered he was no academic – Tarra smiled at this - and left after one year. Having worked constantly since the age of 14 he had money he could use and he decided to travel abroad – to see the sights, and to work, and to learn of other cultures. After five years of backpacking, he arrived in Nepal – and instead of the usual period of time drinking in the aroma of the area before moving on, he felt there was something here which held him in place and he remained, moving into the mountains and insinuating himself into the Nepalese Communities. He had cause to regret one place where he inadvertently crossed paths with a soldier from the Ghurkha Army. Not deliberately and he wasn't being intrusive – more observational – but his studied gaze on this one soldier was enough to antagonize the man and it was only the intervention of a British Colonel which prevented any real harm being inflicted upon him. The Colonel explained how dangerous it would be to get on the wrong side of one of the most effective fighting machines in human form could be. He accepted the Colonel's advice and ventured further into the Nepalese jungles and away from general human contact.

Which was where he met a man who was on his knees and who was either in pain or he was chanting to a tree. Possibly praying.

Nate watched the old man who remained on his knees for a considerable period of time before the man tried standing. When the man stood up, the trauma of being fixed in a single physical position for so long – and there was no way of knowing exactly how long he'd been in this position – the man, elderly in years, lost his balance. He fell to one side and clouted his head on the tree trunk he had been praying to. The injury was enough to open up a wound in his head and he lay there, supine, for some period of time, moaning.

Seeing the man was clearly in pain and seemingly isolated from anyone else, Nate came out from his own place of refuge and offered his assistance to the old man.

At first, there was resistance. The old man was terrified by what he was looking at and Nate wondered if this man, clearly native to this region, who was dressed in very simple robes and no footwear, had ever even seen a Westerner's face before. He took out a flannel, poured cold water on it and gently bathed the bleeding wound. He offered the man a little of the water to drink and some food which had been given to him a day before by a grateful woman who had struggled with a large water container as she carried it up to her home from a stream. He assisted her task – she being suspicious of a foreign face – but showing gratitude when they reached her home and she was safe.

The old man settled and gratefully ate the food, drank the water. Nate showed him a gazeteer Atlas map, pointing out Nepal to him, stating in fragmented Nepalese that this was the old man's country then showed him which country *he* came from by first stabbing himself in his chest with his hand then placing it on the UK. Still befuddled from the wound and shaking from the cold and the wet as rain was a constant in this region, the old man struggled to stand and Nate assisted the man to his feet and the man complied, sensing the young man was no threat to him and he pointed his hands towards a small building across the valley. Nate stared at it and didn't need to ponder on what it was – he'd already been told by other villagers what it was and was then warned to stay away from it.

It was a monastery.

*

The monastery was a mile across the valley and they had to negotiate themselves through a thick tangled forested area to get to it. The old man – apparently a student adept from the monastery – although relatively small in stature and light in weight to begin with - became heavier by the hour it took Nate to reach the front entrance.

Once there, both men fell to the ground from exhaustion.

The light rain was cooling and Nate opened his mouth to drink it in. He did not notice the old man had regained his upright position and had cross a sandy courtyard to reach the entrance door. He pulled on a large metal handle and a bell tolled. The bell alerted Nate and he watched the old man leaning against the wall. After a few minutes the door was opened. The old man was met by another old man dressed in similar robes. This old man called out and three younger men rushed to the door and supported their injured friend. They took him inside. The old man was about to close the heavy wooden door when he saw Nate spread-eagled on the ground. Confusion at first crossed the old man's face and he wondered if this intruder had anything to do with his friend's bloodied condition. He closed the door and then all was silent.

The rain continued to fall and Nate remained where he lay. In truth, he had been holding back on his eating and drinking provisions because he wasn't fully stored with either. He knew from directions given to him by the grateful water-carrier that he was at least ten miles to the next village, provided he kept on this particular road. Well, he had diverted by some considerable margin to bring the old man to this monastery and now it was getting dark. The thunder clouds which moved in this direction indicated the light rain wouldn't remain light for much longer. Through physical exhaustion and depleted provisions, Nate barely had the energy to even stand upright much less cross the valley he had just traversed to bring the old man home.

Home?

In his exhausted state, he actually fell asleep on the sandy courtyard, partially aware of his situation and the rain already landing on him, also aware that he was about to become drenched even more as the dark clouds opened up if he didn't find cover. It is a curious sensation where you are placed betwixt consciousness and sleep, seemingly unable to physically respond to the environment in which you find yourself – despite the possibility of potential dangers.

The rain fell. After a ten-minute pounding which clearly was not going to stop anytime soon, he opened his eyes and searched around the forest to see where he could pitch his tent and at least take refuge from the rain.

As he gazed across the courtyard he became aware now that he was the object of scrutiny from the old man he had seen by the door and three younger men. They too wore similar robes to the man he had aided but theirs was new and cleaner by comparison. He tried to stand but the exhaustion bested him and he fell back. He felt the sensation of being lifted, being carried across the courtyard and was now safe from the cold and the rain, the new welcome sensation of a warm and dry environment, a large stone chamber with many corridors, cloistered in near darkness which were lit only by many candles fixed on the walls and upright standing poles, ringing bell chimes and, all around, an odd aromatic smell which was pleasing to the senses, even soothing and as he was gently transported, he fell unconscious.

*

He woke: confusion raced through his mind because he had no knowledge of where he was or how he had arrived here. He was lain upon a bed of sorts, not built for comfort, a single blanket to protect him from the cold, a small clothed bundle which served as a pillow. He was in a cell of some kind and he wondered if he'd been arrested without remembering why, or what he had done, or if he'd been hurt or had *he* hurt someone? He instinctively ran his hands across his face to shake himself up, open his eyes, get some life in this body – and realised he was bearded. He grabbed the beard by both hands and worked out that this amount of fuzz was at least five, maybe six, days old. How long had been in this place? Who brought him here? What were the charges?

He heard movement outside the cell. Weak from hunger and thirst, he slowly crawled out of this makeshift bed and made for the door. Was it locked? Was he a prisoner? Who were his captors? He opened the door and his questions were answered immediately.

Here, Tarra interrupted. 'You were still in the monastery,' she said and Nate confirmed her assertion.

He stepped out from his cell and saw a number of younger men, all dressed in the same robes and remembered exactly where he was and what these people were. Monks. Many of them saw him but kept their heads down and did not acknowledge him in any way – not even so much as a curious smile.

They were all headed in the same direction and he was about to follow them when a hand rested on his shoulder. He turned, and the old man he'd seen at the door was standing next to the old man he'd carried across the valley. He had a white bandage on his head where the wound had been made and he was smiling. He bowed to Nate, then to the old man who bowed back in return and the bandaged old man walked away, supported by two younger monks.

The old man smiled at Nate and stood back, gesturing for him to walk with him. Nate complied.

*

Nate was taken to another room, up three flights of stairs and across a corridor. If this place was the monastery he'd seen from a distance across the valley it must have hidden a sizeable portion from that distance for the interior was immense. And old. It was made of stone and wooden beams in structure and lit by candles in every corridor. This place had been standing a long time.

The old monk walked Nate to a door, opened it and entered. He bowed to someone in the room and then gestured for Nate to enter. Nate did so – and saw he was a in a large… well, office was the only word he could use to describe where he was standing now – such a room so out of keeping from the rest of the building he had walked through. What he had seen so far was ancient but this room was almost 21st century by comparison. There was an easy armchair to sit upon, a row of books on shelves at least forming a small library. Nate could see the tomes were ancient but well preserved.

And dominating the room was a large ornate wooden desk from which behind another older monk sat. He beamed a welcoming and friendly smile towards Nate and gestured with a nod for the old monk to now leave the room. No words were spoken.

This man gestured for Nate to take his seat on the cosy armchair and Nate complied for he was still exhausted and now, his growling stomach was clearly indicating, he was hungry. He continued to scan the room. A large window gave a panoramic view to the forest beyond and a mountain Nate was meant to climb to reach the next township. Next to the window was an old but still functioning telescope which indicated the man seated at the desk studied astronomy for there were books - written in Nepalese scrawl – which were dedicated to the observation of the stars above.

The door opened and a young monk entered, carrying a tray which held a glass cup which had a reddish-brown liquid in it, obviously hot for steam rose from it. A plate contained food of which kind he could not discern but it looked like flattened breads with a spread of some kind of jam or honey smeared across them.

Not exactly pub grub but Nate was hungry enough to eat anything at this point. The young monk bowed to his superior and exited the room. The senior monk gestured with his hand and Nate studied the food for a few moments – then tucked in.

It was bread of some description – and it was indeed a form of butter spread smeared across the slices – but nothing like Nate had ever tasted before. The reddish-brown liquid may have been tea – but again, nothing like Nate had ever drunk before. He ate and drank the repast and was truly grateful for the food and his hunger had been sated. Assuming the English language was not spoken here – or any other kind of language for that matter as he's heard no-one use the spoken word the entire time he'd been conscious – Nate brought his hands up as if in prayer and bowed his head to indicate his gratitude.

So the next few moments took him completely by surprise.

'And how are you enjoying Nepal, Mister Roden?'

C H A P T E R 1 5
MA TAYARU CHU

Tarra was highly amused.

'He spoke English,' she said. Nate leaned back. He smiled at the retelling of the story, and her reaction, and continued with it.

'Not only English but he was also a very well-spoken linguist. He spoke eight different languages in my presence, only four of which I was able to converse in. I spent the whole day with him. He told me his name was Li Xo and he was a Chinese – but there was always something about him which made me wonder if he was acting under a façade. I learned much from him.'

Nate told Tarra about the origin of the monastery and how it came to be and what religious movement it represented.

'Ever heard of the Kirat Mundum?' he asked. 'The Dharmic religion?' And of course, Tarra shook her head. She barely had time for the more common western religions never mind some abstract movement, probably centuries old, in a country she knew little of beyond the spelling of it.

Nate explained this particular religion though he spared her the specific details of its depth of movement and who the Gods were to whom the natives prayed.

The Kirat was older than Christianity by some many hundreds of years and had been founded by a King Yalamber circa 1779 BC. Nate spared her its journey from that time to the present and stated that this version of the Kirat was of a more recent age – its movements and intentions not wholly in keeping with its antecedents.

85

The more recent version was founded by a Phalgunanda Lingden in 1885 and the man seated before Nate at this time was an actual living descendant of that man.

This version of the Kirat practiced much of the ancestral teachings but, with a few contemporary additions, allow the student adepts to leave the sanctuary of the monastery and go forth into the outside world safe in the knowledge that they could come back once they had tired of what that outside world had to offer.

But their resolve to the movement was a considerable test to undergo and it took many years to reach the days of 'Abandonment' such as it was called if the student adept had chosen to leave.

'What kind of test?' asked Tarra – and that was when Nate presented the branding on his two arms.

Two animals featured on each arm. One was a Bengal Tiger, the other was a Tibetan Wolf.

She studied the marks. Their size was approximately a two-inch square design. The branding design was surrounded by a reddish colouring on his flesh.

'Ma Tayaru Chu,' he explained. She stared at him, not asking him to explain what he had just said but waiting for him to explain it. '*I Am Prepared.*' he told her. She nodded in acceptance of the translation.

'Is that where you learned how to do your Karate?'

He looked at her, a puzzled expression on his face.

'What you did to those two prats Billy set on you the other night. They're both trained in Karate – or some kind of martial arts stuff. You took them out like they were rank amateurs.'

'Well,' he said, 'that's a fair comparison. Compared to the training I undertook, western forms of martial arts are amateurish. They are trained in the basics and, I suppose, to compete in tournaments, wearing graded belts and win cups. What I was taught was how to attack invaders and defend myself against murderers – and in the history of that movement, the monks of yesteryear were forced to learn how to defend themselves.'

He explained how, in the early days of the movement that when the monks of the region were compelled to walk abroad for provisions, water and materials to build they were often attacked by the criminals who were doing the same thing – the difference being they would watch villagers and others actually do the hard work of seeking and finding what they were looking for and then attack them, relieving them of their hard worked-for labours. Following on from the schools of the Sha-Olin and Kara Te teachings, the monks of the Kirat did likewise.

Thus, *MA TAYARU CHU* was born and given life. Unlike the other disciplines, however, which involved spiritual enlightenment to accompany the violent aspect, *MA TAYARUS CHU* was purely conceived to be a form of attack and defence. And in those early days – occasionally even today – monks walking beyond the sanctuary of the monastery would find themselves the subject of marauding thugs who saw them as easy pickings – only to find their own lives held in forfeit when the supposed "victim" retaliated and would overcome the attackers. No law in existence of that region, not then nor now, would dare challenge the inhabitants of the monastery or their mysterious ways.

'Was that painful to do?' she asked, nodding to the brandings. He smiled. He didn't answer that question but instead gave her a thumbnail description of the life he had chosen to undertake.

He told her that he had spent two weeks inside the monastery before he decided this was where he wanted to be for the next period of his life. The ancient teachings and the serenity of this world made him consider the absence of 21st century world pollution and the hell of the world at war with itself and it was a factor he had been entertaining since leaving the UK and since he'd set foot in Nepal and now he knew this place was where he wanted to be.

Tarra stared at him. Seclusion from his own world, his own people, his family (She didn't know what he was running away from and didn't ask) but this was such a gigantic leap from what he knew and where he'd been. She said so.

'I knew it, even then,' he told her 'but the two weeks I was there, learning about the movement, the peace and serenity of mind I had discovered within me… Well, the outside world didn't compare then.'

For seven years then, he resided at the monastery and became a student adept of the Kirat, contemporary and ancient, and he lived in harmony with similar-minded people and the nature of the land which surrounded the region.

'After seven years, the Masters give all student adepts the opportunity to leave the monastery – they call it 'Abandonment' – and go out into the wider world so they can learn for themselves whether they can make their lives work out there – or simply live the life of refuge in the monastery. But if you decide to remain, you can never leave, once you return, you never leave. It's a big ask of people who've been ensconced in this tiny world for nearly all their lives. Many of them have been there since they were younglings – I went there when I was 22 years of age. To them, that is too old to begin their kind of teaching but this man – who'd had a taste of the world – sympathized with my situation and took me in.'

Nate describe then the test each young monk had to endure to pass in order to face the outside world.

'You're taken to a small… tent-like abode, similar to the Wigwams of the American Indians. It is big enough to house six people and once it is closed, everything inside it is trapped. There is a fire burning in a kind of metal brazier in the middle of the tent and that place was a furnace once you'd been standing there for just a few moments. Six Masters are seated, fully-dressed, in an arc and they observe the manners and reactions of the student adept in order to undergo and pass the test. The student is completely naked and his body is covered with some kind of emollient to relax him. There are two stone pillars which the student is roped to and his arms are stretched out wide. Once in that position, you can't escape it. There are two branding irons in the fire and once they are heated long enough, two senior monks take them out – and one at a time, they plunge the irons into each arm. The day I went through the test, there were four other students who attempted it as well.'

Tarra winced. Not familiar with extreme physical pains of any kind she merely recalled the slight pain she felt when the town tattooist put the mark of the Dove on her ankle. It hurt like hell and she'd wished she hadn't fallen for this stunt just to keep in with the other girls. What the branding irons must have felt like when Nate was tied to the stone pillars she could only imagine.

He continued.

'Thing is – being branded isn't the test. The test is how the student adept reacts to the brandings. If he screams, writhes or faints – and they were common reactions to the brandings – then he has failed the test and would not be considered ready enough to leave the monastery. The test was to accept the pain - for only a few moments – without reacting. If you've learned their teachings well enough, the premise is you should be able to withstand such a shock to your physical flesh without demonstrating pain or anger. What it took for me not to scream the place down was some kind of inner strength I never knew I had but I did it. The others didn't. They failed the test. Two fainted, the other two screamed the tent down. They were carried out by other students.'

'Dear God,'Tarra breathed.'What a way to prove your learning.'

'The next step was interesting,'he continued.'One of the Masters then took two towels, drenched of balm liquid which has been soaked in a bath, and wrapped one around each arm. From screaming agony, the balm calms the pain. God knows what is that balm mixture but if the Kirat Masters chose to market it in the West they'd earn a fortune. They wrapped the towelling around my arms and all pain was gone, a kind of throbbing but not much more. The Masters then open the tent and I was released from the ropes. I went outside, still naked, and fell onto the snowy ground. I was there for over an hour under the freezing weather. I felt I was under some kind of hallucination for most of that time until my senses returned and I was able to get up to walk back to the monastery. It was like being drunk and I took over an hour to walk maybe a hundred yards. I lay in bed for three days and then they prepared me with provisions to last two weeks and I left the monastery.'

Tarra listened with care. Obviously, she didn't know if she'd just heard the biggest load of lying baloney she'd ever heard or Nate was telling her a terrible truth. But there was honesty in his voice and she held her own counsel on the story.

The evening came to an end and Nate said it was time for her to go home. She was still in gaze mode when he said it. She had to give herself a shake to realise it was indeed quite late.

A part of Tarra wanted Nate to drive her home in the Aston Martin but instead he walked her back to the Keeper's Lodge. The walk was a little over half an hour and the conversation was general. The one question she wanted to ask, and held back from until they were within visual distance of the Lodge, was how he had travelled from that life of austerity to the obvious wealth he enjoyed today. The house, the car, the grounds… they hadn't come cheap she knew. So how…?

He smiled and told her he had learned how to gamble when walking the Earth and after he had left the monastery behind. It had proved to be profitable in the right company and besides, the monasterial teachings had not forbade it. He became a professional gambler.

She could barely believe he had won so much from the art of gambling to be able to own the house he lived or own an Aston Martin car but she decided no more questions and would raise the subject another time. And now she wanted there to be another time.

Only as they approached the Lodge did she stop him and tell him about her Father's indiscretions. He seemed to either already know about it or was of the opinion such scandalous behaviour was not his business for he did not offer neither sympathetic or condemning remarks. When they were just a hundred yards from the Lodge and out of sight from anyone inside it, she gently took his little finger in her right hand and moved closer to his face. When he did not offer rejection, she kissed him lightly on his mouth.

'What was that test called again?' she asked.

'Ma Tayaru Chu. "*I am prepared*",' he told her. She smiled and then completed the journey to the Lodge alone. When she turned, he was still standing there. She waved to him, he returned the wave and then walked away. Tarra then went inside. She leaned against the door, stared at the ceiling, breathed out and said, 'Christ, what have I just done?'

She locked the door, grateful Mummy and Lainey were in bed and not there to ask a dozen questions as to where she'd been the greater part of the day – she hadn't just been out posting a letter.

The lights were turned off and the Lodge was in complete darkness. After a few moments of night-time silence and with Nate Roden now a good few hundred yards away down the lane, a tree branch was moved aside and a man stepped out from behind it.

He was big – at least six feet four inches and burly – had a face which had clearly seen violence and he wore thick warm clothing along with a woollen hat pulled down almost over his face. He stared at the Lodge – then towards the distant back of Nate Roden. When he turned a corner and was out of sight, the man came out from behind the tree and walked down the same lane.

Only a bored and uninterested owl saw these human events and it wasn't going to tell anyone.

C H A P T E R   1 6
ZEBO PLANS

After their umpteenth row about the plans Zebo had made, Rolfe Tanka stormed out of the main lounge of the Tulse palace. Furious his advice had not been even listened to never mind adhered to, Tanka had been given the duty of preparing the means of travel which would take Zebo Tulse and his comrades out of Albania and across the globe to the country of the United Kingdom.

As far as Bartok, Kursk and Gorovitch were concerned, there was really no problem. In the first place, those men were not the primary concern of Tanka – comrades to Zebo yes, friends maybe, war-like leaders most definitely and in their defence, they had never strayed beyond their own limited borders onto other grounds and especially into Zebo's territory so they were no threat to him.

Secondly, Kursk, Bartok and Gorovitch were seasoned travellers out of Albania. They had holidayed abroad, conducted face-to-face business with other similarly inclined men who had chosen this lifestyle – they had even gone to war abroad. Getting travel permits and Passports for them would be no problem. No - the most remarkable thing here was that Zebo Tulse had never gone abroad. Not for any reason. Further to that, his own personal identity did not even exist on the files of the Law, any legal authority in either Health or Tax departments. To all intents and purposes, Zebo Tulse, like his Father and Grandfather before him, simply did not exist. Getting a Passport for him required the services of the excellent forgers who served the Tulse Empire. But this Passport would have to be the best. A new name and identity, a completely documented and verifiable history and legend in the name Zebo would adopt. Tanka had begged Zebo to allow the comrades to go to the UK and deal with the man who was possibly the assassin of both the Bashkim bastard and Tito – but Zebo refused this advice. This was a matter of honour, Zebo stipulated, many times, to Tanka's face, and honour demanded he deal with this murdering Vagabond personally. And so, defeated in the giving of sound advice, Rolfe Tanka sounded out to his own people as to who the best forger was – then to create this new legend for the man they all served.

Defeated in this argument, and knowing no argument would dissuade Zebo from the course he had set upon, Tanka left the Tulse palace and travelled to Germany. The journey was uneventful and in time, he was put in touch with the Intermediary-Agent Milo Tarn had contacted with regard to Endo's death and an interview was arranged.

The Agent - claiming secrecy and thus ultra-cautious – refused to meet Tanka face-to-face for fear of reprisal against the death of Tito. Tanka assured him this would not be the case and was happy to speak with him under all and any precautions arranged by the Agent. And so, the meeting was made via a 'ZOOM' monitor. The Agent – still cautious – had covered his face and used a vocal discordant to alter his voice. The two men spoke in fluent French and Italian and Tanka really had no idea of the Agent's exact location, or his name or national identity.

He showed the Agent the freeze-frame image of the man who slew Tito and the Agent confirmed this man was the same assassin he had hired to kill Edon Bashkim. That assassination was completed to the entire satisfaction of the employer who had hired him and the mission was paid for upon confirmation of Edon's death by legal authorities. For the life of him, explained the Agent, he could not understand why the assassin was still in Albania two days after Edon's killing and confirmed there was no official sanction on Tito's life – that he knew of. This fight – he watched the whole mobile phone clip – was something he hadn't even been made aware of but out of respect of the name and status of Zebo Tulse, he complied with Tanka's request and freely gave the assassin's codename in this instance – he would attempt to secure the assassin's real name - and possible one of four locations where the assassin could be found. Lyons in France, a small village in Belgium, Berlin in Germany - but only ever in summer apparently…

…and finally, Suffolk in England.

Tanka sent a communique to Zebo. Plan working, information received, will follow up.

*

The following day, the same Agent sent a name, no picture, to Tanka and he confirmed the name as belonging to the man they were looking for.

The name was Nate Roden.

C H A P T E R   1 7

BILLY'S FURY

Tarra woke, fairly confident she had not dreamed of Mister Roden, but his face was the first image which had come to her the moment she had awoken. Even in her still slightly distorted state of mind of half-sleep she was still asking herself why she had kissed the man. She also asked herself to confirm her exact feelings at this time. The one thing she was absolutely certain of – she wouldn't be seeing Billy Telling anymore – well, not as a boyfriend anyway. On this issue, she had given considerable thought.

Her thinking had moved along the lines of exactly what Billy had done when he drove his damn sports car at Phillipa Beddoes when she was riding her horse. Sometime during the night, Tarra had suddenly realised that the horse was one of Max Tierney's mounts and she put a two and two together along the lines of Billy deliberately upsetting a horse already jittery from the noise of road traffic, possibly unseating young Phillipa which in turn could possibly result in the Tierney stable getting a bad name, maybe a lawsuit against the Tierney Equine Farm for negligence against them in favour of the child seated upon the horse – resulting in legal action taken against the Tierney's by the Beddoes family – the Tierney's being taken to Court, losing their license to run the farm…

Tarra couldn't understand why she hadn't twigged it before. Neither Billy nor his Father had shown any kind of remorse for the speeding car stunt and under normal circumstances that stunt would've met with a stern reproof from the Father – but nary a word or rebuke followed this time and Billy wasn't even apologetic about what he had done.

Her conclusions were possibly thin in the absence of absolute evidence – but just the notion of Billy doing what he had done *just for fun* was enough for her to make her decision to dump the immature man today. She sat upright on her bed for ten minutes mulling over this decision.

Her Mother brought up a tray of tea and biscuits for both Tarra and Lainey who, at 08.00 hours, was still asleep in bed. She and five friends had held a slumber party in the Lodge shed – a sizeable construction in the back garden – and Sasha had had to go the slumber-ites at 02.30 hours to tell them to pack their noise in and get some sleep. As she returned to her own bed, Sasha could hear the five friends and her Daughter laughing their heads off. Somehow, during the early morning, all the slumber-ites had entered the house, silently, and had finished up in a dead sleep in Lainey's own bed which was just about big enough to contain all six of them. Sasha hadn't heard a thing so stealth had been employed which, coming from a gang of laughing noisy 12-year olds, she considered an impressive feat. It deserved tea and breakfast in bed.

Tarra told her Mother of her intention to give Billy his marching orders, even citing the Beddoes horse incident as reason for doing so. Sasha was immensely relieved as she truly did not like the Telling's and Billy in particular. A blowhard loudmouthed bully and an altogether too unpleasant a character who really was not good enough for Tarra's kind of person.

How Billy would take the news however, was another matter…

Once the six delinquents had been given their breakfast repast, Sasha returned to Tarra's room and asked how she'd spent the previous evening because she hadn't come home by the time she, Sasha, had retired to bed.

Now Sasha already knew Tarra was heading out to Haydock's Barn to deliver a letter of apology regarding Billy's actions which she had written to this Mister Roden person – she still didn't really know him well enough to address him by his Christian name – and that letter, once posted, would have been the work of a moment and she should have been home before mid-afternoon. She mentioned this in passing.

Tarra breathed out and marshalled her thoughts. Exactly what to tell her Mother about the story – which she was still doubting in her mind – Mister Roden had given her.

She relayed the story as best she could remember. She even included the gambling aspect of the story which apparently had allowed Mister Roden the comfort he was currently enjoying by residing in his house of opulence for Sasha was aware of the new abode at Haydock's so it was obvious money was involved. The design of the house, the layout of the garden, the car. Yes, Mister Roden was clearly rolling in it, but - was the house his? Was the car his? Was the money which rebuilt the whole area his? Gambling was a possibility to be sure but this place must have cost over a million – more likely two million – and that would mean one hell of a gambling addiction for very few gamblers win so often or so much that they can afford to live off their winnings. And at this point, no-one knew exactly what other industry or profession Mister Roden was employed in.

The one aspect Sasha was hearing for the first time was the mini fracas which had taken place inside The Keys Pub on the night of Phillipa's birthday. This was news. How Mister Roden had dealt with the two men – Sasha had seen them, knew who they were – sounded quite impressive. Exactly what he would have done to Billy had Tarra not intervened was also an interesting point. Sasha knew the two men by reputation and their fighting abilities were widely known for they frequently showed up in the sports pages of the Suffolk Echo relating to Martial Arts Tournaments and how successful they were. For this man, Roden, to so easily overcome them with a small demonstration of his own fighting abilities was a matter for concern. And the story of how he had acquired those fighting abilities seemed too high and flighty for Sasha to accept at face value.

Still didn't explain why Tarra had stayed out so late.

Tarra went on to describe the house and how fantastic it seemed to her. Like a fairy tale kind of house and fairy tale kind of garden. Any man who could carve out a garden for the benefit of the beasts of the Earth had her vote, she said, and Sasha decided not to push out any more doubts concerning Mister Roden. No sense in prejudicing her case. She asked if he had brought her home in his car and Tarra said he had walked her to the Lodge. She did not mention the kiss.

And then the Lodge doorbell went.

It was Lainey, still dishevelled from her deep sleep, who came into Tarra's bedroom, slowly climbed onto Tarra's bed, wrapped her arms around her elder Sister and said 'The loser is outside,' informing them both that Billy was standing on the porch, angry, and ringing the bell again.

Having already announced to her Mother of her intentions, Tarra downed her tea and put on her dressing gown. Sasha said she would come with her but Tarra held her hand up and Sasha remained on Tarra's bed, Lainey's head now in her lap and, unbelievably, asleep again.

Sasha could hear the conversation but only a hubbub of it – until she heard Billy's voice rising most clearly and sounding furious. He demanded to know why - more hubbub from Tarra – and Billy's voice raised even louder. Now he was protesting. Loud protests. Tarra was keeping her voice level in her explanations but Billy was losing it big time. He was now in the front garden remonstrating to her, how he had remained loyal to her after all her other friends had deserted her when Daddy performed his magical disappearing act and taking the bimbo bitch with him along with tons of everybody else's money.

Sasha had gently lain the sleeping Lainey down on Tarra's bed and had moved to the front bedroom where the five children, now fully awake, had been disturbed by the loud voices below and were watching two adults shouting at each other, hammer and tong. Well only the bloke was at it hammer and tong, the girl was standing still, her arms crossed and still dressing in her dressing gown.

'Oh my God,' said Olyvia, 'that's Lainey's Sister.'

They hadn't heard Sasha entering the room and so didn't register her when she was standing next to them and watching Billy Telling – 'Never liked him,' said Ellee – red-faced with fury lashing out at her with his hands though still not making physical contact with her person.

Sasha watched – concerned. Tarra was more than a match for Billy Telling when it came to a verbal spat – but not if it descended to something physical. She hadn't been trained for that possibility in her life.

And Billy was now in full blown eruption mood – and Evie said to them all, 'He's a mad sod, Billy Telling – I saw him kick a dog once and then have a go at the dog owner for letting him off his lead. They were on the field for God's sake.'

Billy now walked to the front gate of the garden and literally kicked it off its hinges sending it across the road. He stormed through the gate entrance and turned back to continue his tirade, his arm outstretched and an accusing finger pointed at Tarra…

…when he suddenly stopped.

Not only stopped but the fury vanished from his face – and he wasn't looking at Tarra anymore. He stood still, an expression of query and confusion on his face. His hands went to his hips as if he were asking a question of someone and not believing the answer being given back.

'Why's he stopped?' asked Rubee.

The answer walked into view. The girls craned their heads to see the man who had just joined the fray. He wore a black leather short jacket, black T shirt, black trousers and black trainers.

'Ooh,' the girls chorused. A man in black. Standing in the space between the screaming enemy and the oppressed Princess. How romantic.

'Who's that?' asked Olyvia.

A pause – no answer from any of the slumber-ites because none of them had ever seen Nate Roden before. So the answer came from Mrs Browne who apparently had been standing there and none of them had seen her.

'His name is Nate Roden,' she said. 'He recently moved into the area.'

Evie shouted. 'Oh… he's the man who stopped Philly Beddoes from being turfed onto her arse… her back… I mean… when she was on her horse.' Sasha confirmed that observation.

They all stared at the confrontation below, though now it had become more a tableau because none of them were moving. Billy was speaking.

'What's he saying?' asked Ellee.

'He's saying "I'm not scared of you",' said Libbi, not a lip reader but in fact, that actually was what Billy was saying to Nate Roden.

'For someone who's not scared he's backing off quite a few paces,' said Evie.

Billy had now backstepped at least ten yards away from Nate Roden who had stopped by the now demolished gate entrance and hadn't advanced since.

The fury of Billy Telling's attitude had been subdued and frustrated, impotent, aware that he was in line for a possible thrashing because, God knows, he couldn't even do what Boley and Robinson could and look how easily they'd been planted onto the floor.

Despairingly, Billy turned on his heels and walked away. Parked some distance away from the Lodge, the MG sports car awaited its owner to leap into it without opening its doors, ignite it and then speed it away down the thin lane at speeds never designed for this kind of road. This was its owner's usual manner.

But not today.

Billy walked back to the car, opened the driver door though he could have easily have just popped his leg over the door and simply sink into the seat. The car was started but its engines did not rev and it was driven, at a road speed of 30 mph, away from the Lodge and all was quiet again.

The girls frowned. Were they expecting a fist fight between the local thug named Billy Telling and the total stranger whose name they had already forgotten? The door opened and a sleepy-eyed Lainey entered the room, climbed into bed and within seconds was sound asleep.

'We're gonna have to train Lainey how to last longer in a slumber party,' said Ellee.

The incident was not quite finished. The man in black was handing a small pouch to Tarra. She took it, smiled and said 'Thank you,' to the total stranger and Libbi translated it for the girls. He then walked away. Tarra came back into the house and Sasha exited the room. The girls then joined Lainey on her bed but not in sleep – the excitement they had just witnessed was too much for them.

Sasha walked down the stairs with quiet movements. She saw Tarra holding onto her pouch bag which she had clearly taken with her when she went to post the apology letter and had clearly forgotten to take with her when she left. How kind of Mister Roden to bring it all the way to her door.

It was the way Tarra was holding the pouch bag which concerned Sasha. As if it were something precious which had been salvaged from a fire or a cave filled with angry man-eating animals. The man who'd brought it back to her was her hero and she would adore him for the rest of her life.

Tarra was now aware she was the focus of her Mother's attention. She dropped her eyes away from her Mother's gaze.

'Don't ask, Mummy,' she said.

CHAPTER 18
JOURNEY TOWARDS DEATH

At the International airport of Tirana, six men shifted uneasily in the company of so many Police Officers. Not that any Police Officer would so much as even speak to them for all the visible Law Enforcement Officers were aware of who these men were and why they were here in the airport though not the reason why they were leaving Albania and had been given the strictest instructions by their superiors to note their presence, and their exit, and do nothing more.

For Bartok, Kursk, Gorovitch, Tanka and Davidoff this journey was a par-for-the-course near every week event. For Zebo, it was border-line terrifying. He couldn't remember the last time he'd been this far from home and the sight of the large crowds had even disturbed his otherwise tranquil state of mind. He was a man who enjoyed the wide-open spaces of Albanian countryside where you could count the amount of people you would see in a single week on one hand and still not require the whole five digits. His eyes never left the milling crowds – viewing them as an intrusion. Tanka had even begged Zebo to charter a private hire plane so that this party could travel in relative peace and quiet and not be under the scrutiny of the airport's Security Officers and their CCTV cameras who may not have been made aware of how important Mister Tulse and his party were. But again, Zebo restrained his Advisor's pleas and chose this method of transport instead. Tanka stared at his Patrone's wide-eyed expressions as he watched the crowding people and wondered if he'd regretted making this choice of travel, or even making this journey at all.

The trouble with being a solitary soul, demanding social exclusion from the masses, is that when such a thing as travelling this way happens either by accident or by design, a form of xenophobia creeps into the person's psyche. In this airport, practically every culture

102

and race were represented and to a life-long seasoned bigot like Zebo Tulse who viewed the rest of the world's human species as a cesspit of filth, fit only for him to use as slaves or prostitutes or people who would kill on his behalf, die even, for him, serving him in the same way as a subjugated race would to a beloved or much feared King.

These people did not know him, probably never even heard of him, did not know what he did or had done to live, did not know his history or what made him the man he is. To all intents, he was as much a nonentity to them as they all were to him. For a man who believed he ruled in his world it was an object lesson to him to know he didn't. This world was much bigger than he'd believed. Tanka wondered if Zebo was drinking this assimilation in.

The plane taking them to the first part of their journey was announced and they all trundled along the directed lines put on the floor by the airport. Tanka prayed no officious Security Officer would request of them to answer a few questions about their journey or what was in their suitcases. Strategy and pragmatism had been observed and Tanka had made absolutely certain that none of the party would carry any kind of weaponry at all. Not so much as small pen-knife which young Mister Davidoff was apt to use. The weapons they would eventually require would be provided by the many gangs of Albanian origins already placed inside the British borders.

An hour later, the plane rose into the sky. Zebo was asleep within minutes. Hardly surprising, Tanka thought, he'd not slept more than three hours in the past thirty-six.

United Kingdom, here we come.

*

Tanka sat back and closed his eyes. Not for need of sleep or relaxation – he was anything but relaxed – but for the venture ahead which he believed his Patrone was anything but suited for. In all his life, Zebo Tulse had led in violence but had never actually killed a man himself. He had grown up around violent people who either fought the wars in person or directed the wars from a safe distance. His Father, Jante, had never killed either but Grandfather Zelke had, many times, personally taken other men's lives. Tanka did not know the exact number – such attention to detail had never been a matter of consideration in those early days when one faction of attrition had decided to wage conflict upon another. The aim was to shed blood – as much as the enemy's blood as was possible – rid the faction of its leading heads, assimilate those who wished to live into the victorious winning side and continue this terrible way of living in order to survive. With technology and modernised warfare to be found at the touch of a computer button of the warmonger's fingertips, the wars became even more bloody and widespread. It was only ever a question of which faction had the steel to inflict the greatest harm regardless of consequence.

The Bartok's, the Kursk's, the Gorovitch and Bashkim Families were powerful to be sure but it was the Tulse Family which held the upper ground in practically every conflict and in their victories, they would gain more ground and people.

And now this damn nonsense. Zebo had had it rammed into his head by the ghosts of his Father and Grandfather, that his Son's death, and the vengeance which must follow it, was a matter of honour and he alone must be the man to pull the death trigger against the assassin. But ordering a man's death and actually conducting it are two separate matters and Tanka – though convinced of his Patrone's courage and intelligence – was not convinced he had the will to do this thing.

All had been prepared at the London end. They would be met – not physically – by Brothers of the Tulse Family who had secured a living in the UK practicing extortion, slavery and prostitution and had sworn to continue serving the Tulse line. They would acknowledge their Patrone's entry into the country and then follow them to a place of safety where the matter of weapons would be dealt with.

The Agent who had passed on the assassin's details confirmed their man had indeed been in Lyons in France, in Gent in Belgium and in Berlin, Germany. These visits were apparently recreational and not professional. His main place of residence, however, was in a County named Suffolk, East Anglia in England. The man's address had already been supplied and observation of him and his coming and going was already long under way.

The plane whined a descending noise and the tannoy system announced they were approaching Heathrow Airport. Tanka stole another glimpse to his Patrone. Zebo Tulse – gangster, warmonger, the man who ordered other people's deaths and stole their money by providing those people with unasked for services - had the look of absolute terror on his face. A man in his late seventies who had never flown on a plane before. What a way to begin.

Three hours after leaving Tirana airport, the plane landed at Heathrow.

Now the real journey to death would begin.

CHAPTER 19
ABSENCE MAKES THE HEART GROW...

In the four days following the unsettling episode with Billy Telling, Tarra kept a relatively low profile in going out for fear of running into him, or his Father or their many friends. The Telling's were still a high-profile name and family in this area and the Browne name - though not totally tainted, people did not hold Sasha responsible for Edmund's actions - was still a name not to be completely trusted. Sasha had found that fact out early on when it came to mixing society functions with business and money. Sasha had indeed been replaced on a number of sub-committees where fiscal business was prominent and was side-lined into smaller areas of whatever that particular function was.

Tarra learned a similar lesson. Before the day was out, she had received a number of phone calls from 'friends' making enquiries about the Billy incident. Now she hadn't breathed a word of the incident to anyone – actually not even to her Mother as the subject was off-radar the moment the door was closed. Each of Lainey's friends had older sisters and obviously they had told them about the incident. From there, the rumour mill had flown into over-drive for by mid-afternoon, Tarra had received over a dozen calls from friends who demanded to know not just the *full-skinny* on what happened but who was the mysterious 'man-in-black' who had come to her aid and was he the same bloke who'd saved young Phillipa Beddoes from being thrown off the horse?

'Yep,' answered Tarra and gave each of them very limited info on the stranger though for personal reasons did not mention the fact that she had kept company with said hero the night before nor the kiss which ended their night.

More calls followed and Tarra put the phone on 'answer-phone' only and turned her mobile off. She spent the next day searching for employment. An arduous task normally but today, a blessing by comparison.

Two days passed and Tarra was now very aware that cars were passing by the Lodge – situated some distance away from the main road – and the cars were constantly at speed with horns blaring. Not Billy's car because his horn had a very distinctive sound but it was obvious the word had gone out and equally obvious Billy's mates were taking up the cudgels on his behalf. Driving past the Lodge, engines revving, horns blaring, practically every ten minutes. Tarra suffered these intrusions in silence but hoped like hell the nonsense would stop before Mother came home from Lowestoft where she had gone with Lainey to visit relatives. She also considered paying a visit to Mister Roden to see if he could make some kind of noise on her behalf to put an end to the intrusions but thought better of it. At the moment, she thought, it's nuisance value and Billy isn't worth a Police interview never mind actual Police time in a cell just because a bit of nonsense got out of hand.

After the third evening had worn in, the cars and their silliness disappeared and Tarra made an excuse to take a walk for the evening as she'd been inside most of the day.

It was still fairly early and as she approached the surrounding fence she could see the gates were locked. There was no sound coming from within the compound – not the thumping sound of Mister Roden exercising, not music from inside the house. It was a warm night and she considered he would have a window open here and there but no sound reached her ears.

Feeling stupid and childish, she skimmed up the tree which offered the best view of the compound – the same one Billy had climbed – and saw the house and the compound was in complete darkness. She recalled, when Mister Roden had taken her home that night, there were security lights placed all around the fencing, some in the trees and some on the house. Nothing was beaming tonight. Mister Roden was not at home.

Feeling low, she trudged all the way back home. This was the fourth night she hadn't seen him since he'd returned her pouch-bag. He'd enquired to see if she was alright following Billy's tirade which he'd witnessed for some time before intervening but had not taken it too far out of respect to the Browne family. What he would do at a later time and on other premises was anybody's guess and Tarra wanted to assure him she was fine and please don't take this any further, he isn't worth it but she would tell him this later and in private – preferably in his house.

She wondered all the way home whether or not the act of kissing him had been a wise thing to do. She'd kissed a near total stranger after all. She knew nothing about him at all beyond the story he'd given her. A reclusive to be sure. Adrift from his family, backpacking across the globe, settling in a monastery with a bunch of monks, learning dubious skills then branching out to become an international gambler who'd won zillions at Poker and was able to afford this fairy tale castle. Now that she'd aired that story-line out, she knew she knew as little about him now as she did when he was in his car waiting for the horses to go by. So, evaluate the situation. One: He is much older than I am. Two: He may be married and is waiting for his Wife to join him from wherever she is hiding – but he hadn't mentioned a wife and if ever there was a home that screamed "*I am a bachelor*" it was the one where she'd spent a whole afternoon and a sizeable chunk of evening. No signs of anyone else living there, no photographs of wife or family – actually, no photographs at all now that she'd mulled over that thought. Finally, 3: Maybe his sexual preference was not for the female. That prospect upset her.

Why?

She had never believed in love at first sight but there was something happening here and it disturbed her. Okay, she considered, he is kind of good looking in some unconventional way. But Tarra knew when she thought "good-looking", she was thinking of a young Brad Pitt, or Leonardo "whatsisface" when he was dying on the Titanic ice berg. Someone whose physical facial visage was striking her senses immediately upon first glance and Mister Roden's face hadn't struck her that way.

Not then.

Mummy had used a word when describing a man she had known back in the days when she was courting Daddy. Not conventionally attractive she explained but… he was… "Enigmatic". What the hell is that, Mummy, asked Tarra, then only 17 years old. Basically, Mummy continued, if someone is "Enigmatic" then it means you can't put your finger on what exactly it is that makes him attractive to you – but you *are* attracted to them and that was pretty much the way Tarra was feeling now thinking about Mister Roden.

That was it, then. Mister Roden was an "Enigmatic". She looked the word up in the Collins Dictionary and its definition matched Mister Roden perfectly.

Can you fall in love with an enigma?

She walked home. If she walked in one direction, it was a straight one-mile trek to the Lodge. If she diverted at this particular point, it would take longer – and also take her past Billy's farm.

Out of funk and foolishness, Tarra chose the long path – the wrong path.

She was within a hundred yards of the farm when she heard the revelry noises. Four cars were parked on the road and she knew two of them. Who did they belong to now…?

Oh yes, Timbo and… someone called Ellison. The other two she wasn't certain of but she knew she'd seen these cars screeching past her home a few days ago.

So…

She knew she'd made a mistake passing this way and decided to backtrack her steps and go all the way around. The walk would be longer, she would get home maybe an hour later – but at least safer.

She turned… and the man standing behind her frightened the wits completely out of her mind.

'Well well,' said Marc Ellison, 'what do we have here?'

*

Furious at her stupidity, Tarra violently protested to Billy, Ellison, the prick named "Timbo" and four other pieces of human garbage who saw life as an excuse to do what they were doing right at this very moment; getting blasted out of their minds on foot-long spliffs and booze and chastising the girl who had the effrontery to dump their mate Billy like he was nothing more than a dog-turd.

And it wasn't restricted to verbal chastisement either. Tarra knew the reputation of at least one of the four men whose name she couldn't recall and it involved the beating of a young girl who had rejected his drunken fumbling. It had ended up in Court but he was looked upon by a kindly Magistrate who told the Court that the Defendant was "basically a good soul who'd allowed the poison of alcohol to cloud sensible judgement, resulting in this sad case which could possibly be injurious to a glowing future should he not learn from this lesson." Verdict: a desultory Fine, a stern rebuke and off he went from Court laughing his head off for so easily gulling an old fossil with too much faith in human nature.

And Billy did not attempt to dissuade the group to give Tarra an easy time – in fact, his contributions barely made any worthwhile volume compared to the ranting screaming issued from his mates.

But Tarra was now in fear for her well-being. These bastards meant business and their business was all about harming the woman who had humiliated her boyfriend – and yes, they knew of the incident at The Keys regarding Boley and Robinson. So, they demanded, who's the guy with the fancy moves? Who interfered with Billy's plan to teach the man a few lessons? Who's the man in black they demanded to know.

This chastisement went on for some fifteen minutes – and fifteen minutes in a threatening environment is a long time.

She was now pinned against the gate. The seven men crowded her, making silly advancing steps, throwing small projectiles at her, nothing too big or solid but the menace spoke loud and clear…

…and so did the sudden silence when they were just a few yards away from her.

Silence – and then staring. Not at her though. Over her shoulder. What on Earth…?

Slowly, she moved from the gate and turned back to see what they were looking at. Well, she thought, it's the "man in black". How timely.

But his face. She'd never seen a face like it. Yes, it was Mister Roden - but his face…

Dear God, she thought, *I'm* terrified – what the hell must they be feeling like?

Billy spoke first. 'That's him,' he blurted out. 'That's the bastard who tumbled Boley and Robbie.'

Ellison took a step towards Tarra – 'Well…' he said, threateningly, and if it was his intention to speak any more threatening words he didn't get the chance to do so for Mister Roden leapt the gate using its top bar as leverage, landing on his two feet and then swirling around and kicking him across the face, which sent him crashing into a wooden barrel.

A "Roundhouse" kick I think that's called, Mister Ellison, thought Tarra, but I may be wrong.

Timbo grabbed the first long-handled implement to hand – a pitchfork. He used it as a soldier would use a bayoneted rifle, stabbing towards Mister Roden as if he were the national enemy or a sandbag. And as he stabbed forward, Mister Roden stepped forward and kicked the pitchfork between its sharpened prongs and Timbo was sent flying backwards at least ten yards, landing in some muck deposited by a horse and not cleaned up by the Telling farm-hand – or better known as: Billy.

A minor pause followed. Four men stood quite still while Billy edged backwards, trying to get out of sight. Two of the four simultaneously launched themselves at Mister Roden and he grabbed one of them by the lapels of his jacket and kicked out at the other man who copped the kicked under the chin and was sent crashing into a wheelbarrow. Not unconscious but definitely not interested in any more activity tonight. The man Nate had hold of suddenly broke down and crumbled to his knees, seemingly begging for another chance. As Nate released him, the miscreant suddenly grabbed Nate by the legs and screamed at his fellow fighters to assist him. Nate pulled his hair back and stabbed him in the eye with his fingers. He screamed, this time for real and let Nate go. He crawled away, still screaming.

Without waiting for the other two hesitant dullards to make their move, Mister Roden jumped towards them and simultaneously punched both of them in their faces and both of them hit the ground and stayed down. A possible mix of the booze and recreational drugs and a heavy dose of violence ended their futile attempts at violence.

Which left Billy Telling who was still backing away, a look of total fear on his face. He stumbled onto yet another farming implement – a garden fork – and he snatched it up. He tried to look menacing but in Tarra's eyes he just looked pathetic. If Billy hadn't twigged yet that any kind of weapon against this man Roden was as much use as trying to stop a raging fire by peeing on it.

Roden stood still and Billy appeared frozen in the moment.

It was call from behind them which halted the fracas. William Telling appeared – in his dressing gown – and shouted to Billy to put the fork down. Billy didn't move. William then crossed the dirty courtyard – he wasn't even wearing slippers - and stood between Billy and Mister Roden. The expression on his face didn't quite match Mister Roden's but it was a pretty good try.

'Put it down. Pack this bloody nonsense up and get your drunken friends away from here. They can leave the cars here. Do it now.'

Billy remonstrated, more out of humiliation than courage – for the third time and again in front of Tarra, he had been bested by this bloody man and this was his only chance to restore matters.

A pause: and then William struck his Son across the side of his heads with an open hand. He clouted him a second time and Billy lost purchase of the makeshift weapon. The look of total astonishment he levelled at his Father was extraordinary for William Telling had never corrected his Son's foolishness in such a way before. A physical rebuke, in front of witnesses, and Billy was now reduced to the state of Pathetic. Even Tarra felt a momentary sadness for him. Mister Roden maintained his stance.

William Telling turned to Tarra. 'I am so sorry, Tarra. I will sort this. My Son will never bother you again.' He then turned to Mister Roden and addressed him in that way. 'Mister Roden, I know you are a man of power and I would be grateful if you allow me to deal with this. It doesn't need to get worse, does it?'

And at this genuine gesture of common sense, there was a cessation of violence. Mister Roden demonstrated compassion. He paused, began to walk to Tarra, then turned back and walked to William and shook his hand. Then William opened the gate – clearly not expecting anyone else to do it and not expecting Tarra to leap over it, watched Tarra and this man Roden leave the Telling Farm.

Two hundred yards away from the Farm and now out of their sight and sound, Tarra broke down. She sobbed into Mister Roden's jacket coat and wrapped her arms around him. 'I was scared,' she cried and the realisation that it was partly her fault had upset her maybe even more.

She cried for ten minutes, the tears and heaving body diminishing between gaps. She shivered in his embrace for now at this time of the year it was beginning to edge towards the autumn period. He took his jacket off and placed it around her. She held onto it with both hands crossing her torso, then she put her arms through the sleeves. It looked silly and large on her but God it was warm. She looked up at his face, the tears streaking her make-up down her face.

'I went to your place,' she said. 'It was in darkness.'

They walked to his car which was parked a short distance away. He told her he'd been in London the past four nights as he was engaged in a card-gambling competition. A lot of money was at stake and he'd come out of it rather well.

So, she thought, he's still tripping that part of the story out. She didn't know whether to believe him or not but didn't say so out loud. So how did he just turn up here tonight?

He'd seen a vixen fox and her three cubs crossing the lane and he'd stopped to let them pass when he heard screaming. He parked his car and investigated the sounds and observed the drunken thugs for long enough to know what was going on. When his own name was invoked, he knew it was she who was being chastised. Then he intervened.

She looked up at him – his face was now back to the normal state she knew him as but now she wondered about his anger. The kick towards Ellison was smart and his defensive move against Timbo took courage. Luckily, she said, they were all halfway high to the Moon on their druggie and boozy party – taking them out must have been made easier for that reason. He replied and told her if they'd been more capable he would've hit them in a different way. She believed him.

Another pause – and then she wrapped her arms around his neck and kissed him passionately. This time, it was a genuine kiss – not a peck between friends - and he did not push her away. They stood there below the shining Moon and kissed each other as though they really were lovers and no interfering boyfriend or Mother could possibly have parted them.

Not that she needed reminding – she'd seen him in his exercise work-out on the mannequin – but God *damn*, she thought, this man is hard to the touch. His body was flexed – probably still recovering from the bout of physical exertions just demonstrated – and she felt safer now than she'd ever felt before.

Eventually the kiss ended but she still maintained her embrace and he did not attempt to prise her away from his body.

In keeping with the company of the gambler, she gambled.

'I don't want to go home,' she said. 'I want to stay with you.'

She didn't look up at him because she did not want to see an expression of doubt or disapproval on his face upon this suggestion. She held him even tighter. He stroked the back of her head. Slowly then, he took her face and stared at her, wiping the streaks away from her cheeks and said 'Let's go, then.'

He opened the car door and she climbed inside. He drove up the lane and reached the junction. If he turned left, she was going back to the Lodge – if he turned right, he was going to Haydock's Barn.

He turned right.

C H A P T E R 2 0
A GREETING OF ARMS

In order to keep the journey as unobtrusive as possible, to blend in with scores of other travellers who had just left Heathrow Airport, Tanka ordered two taxis to take them to Liverpool Street Train Station and from there, it would be an hour's journey on the train to Ipswich. The six men who had waited for them at the Airport lounge did likewise and also took the train to reach Ipswich. At Ipswich Station the six men who served Zebo Tulse took two cars and drove out of the station car park – all very calm and with no apparent reason for the CCTV cameras to mark them out as being suspicious – driving the cars just a short distance up the road and then allowing their guests from Albania to catch up with them and get into the cars – again with no obvious reasons to mark them out as being different to the common herd – there was no shouting of names, no Albanian language spoken, no meet or greet movements made. Once inside the cars, the visitors were then taken to the place called The Heath.

Zebo enjoyed this part of the trip. It was countryside. He enjoyed looking at the English countryside. It reminded him of home. They arrived at a large area of fields and forestry and a small picnic arrangement area. They even brought a picnic hamper to pass the day, blend in with others doing the same thing, as there would be no action until later that night.

As they ate, one man sat aside from the others and Zebo joined him. This man was the Head liaison between Albania and England and was one of Zebo's oldest and trusted friends – both had served Zebo's Father in some really gruesome surges against the family enemies when young and each had saved the other's life. The man – Riko Varon – was an actual soldier while Zebo was a planner of war-like movements but,

116

historically, at one point, a bomb had been planted at the large country home where they made their plans in and had successfully killed eight of the Tulse army – Varon was injured but had the strength and courage to carry out Zebo – also injured – from the demolished building and to safety. This action was gratefully acknowledged by Zebo's Father, Jante, and Varon was rewarded. He and Zebo then planned and carried out a revenge assault on the perpetrators of the bomb attack and the friendship was cemented in blood.

It was Varon who had been keeping nightly vigils on the man Roden's home while his soldiers alternated during the daylight hours. He described it as he had seen it from the same tree Billy and Tarra had climbed – he had even watched them do it. He informed Zebo of this apparent current relationship with a village girl and asked if it would present any difficulty. Killing this man Roden was a given task to be sure but what if bystanders were involved? Zebo ordered the man's destruction was all he had come here to do and no-one else was to be harmed unless circumstances intruded and it was necessary. So far, Varon told Zebo, apart from nights when the man Roden had not slept at his own home, he had shown little interest in being anywhere else. This girl was a new thing. Recently, he had been away for four nights – Varon didn't know where or what the business was - but he was at home now.

They waited until other picnickers left the area and then secured the whole encampment while they brought out the weapons of choice. The six soldiers were given the task of securing Roden's exterior at his home, but not to enter the home itself. This would be accomplished by the physical removal of the fence gates by a small explosion and he, Zebo, accompanied by Kursk, Gorovitch, Bartok and the Bashkim operative, Davidoff, would then attack the house itself. Here, Varon informed Zebo the house gave an impression of looking normal but was, in fact, very well-protected.

An expert in such matters of security, Varon outlined the differing systems which had been placed around the house. CCTV cameras were a given but there were tripwires and beam lights which could only be seen if the intruder was wearing a special kind of spectacle arrangement. Climbing the fence would appear to be easy with the correct tools but at the top of the fence, opposite sides of the whole length, there were well constructed and well-hidden cameras which beamed a light across. Anyone climbing over the fence would break the beam and, in all probability, a silent alarm would sound, alerting the Police – not just locally but also the main station based in Ipswich – for, Varon guessed, anyone employing this kind of protection, would also be guarded by the Police.

Zebo listened and understood. It was his intention to make this a clean and quick kill. Maybe even attack Roden before he had managed to gain refuge into his home and not give him the opportunity to sound the alarms at all. He just wanted the man dead – pure and simple – it would not a be a bloody duel between Titans he joked. He had already given Tanka instructions to pass onto Varon and his men once the invasion had commenced which would give the Police, the Fire Service and the Ambulance service enough work to be getting on with.

The weapons which had been brought, were broken down in separated segments and the men working under Varon were even now putting the separated segments together. His only query was the identity of the outsider who he knew did not belong to the Tulse Family – Davidoff.

Here, Zebo Tulse was circumspect. He confirmed Davidoff's identity and whom he served in Albania – then told Varon exactly what Davidoff's fate was to be. His surliness, his arrogance and continued fidelity to Vanna Bashkim was a reason for concern and Zebo had decided Davidoff would fall here – along with the Roden man. Maybe even implicating the Bashkim servant in the murder of the Englishman. Varon gave his consent for this decision to his Patrone.

The weapons set and concealed, Varon made the instructions very clear: the home was to be invaded if the man Roden was there, and with very little pause, he continued, Roden was to be executed – by Zebo Tulse ALONE!!! If there were witnesses, unfortunate, but possible, they would be dealt with by Kursk, Gorovitch and Bartok. Varon and his men would remain outside the perimeter gates to ensure no unfortunate soul would be passing at the wrong moment, to witness or hear the slaughtering of Nate Roden and attempt to report it to the Police prematurely.

It was now, as the men approached their respective cars, when Zebo showed Varon the same mobile images seen by all his comrades and Varon expressed doubts about the images.

'Patrone,' he said, 'I see this man, every day.' He used Nate Roden's name but pronounce it as "Natty Rodden". 'I know his face as I know the back of my hand, as I know your face, Patrone. And I know this man I see every day is not the man I am seeing on the phone.'

And this disturbed Zebo Tulse, for Davidoff had already confirmed the man on the phone was also not the man who had halted him and the other two bodyguards the day Endo Bashkim was murdered. So, not the killer of Endo or Tito, and yet the information given by the Intermediary-Agent was so precise. Perhaps, he considered, this man was a third player in the two assassinations. The man with the gun which killed Endo – and then somehow involving himself with the murder of Tito for the real killer did not fly from the area – there must have been transport to spirit him away from the village. Perhaps Nate Roden was just one of a group. This may necessitate a conversation between himself and Roden before he was put to death, Zebo thought.

But now it was late and they must travel to the man's home.

CHAPTER 21
INVASION

The first part of the grand plan fell apart the moment they arrived at Nate Roden's home. By general accord, none of the sentinels guarding the Roden residence were allowed to use their phones to alert the others that Roden was not at home in case their messages were overheard and traced by the lawful authorities. It was suggested that if this man had gone to such lengths to protect his home with such elaborate technologies it followed the use of phones to send and receive even coded messages could be used against them should their capture occur. Never assume the Law cannot operate in an efficient way when in pursuit of a criminal or their gang. Zebo had been fascinated by the outstanding downfall of an American President – the Leader of one of the most powerful nations in the world – because tape recordings had implicated the President's Office and the man himself. Citing this example, Zebo argued if nothing was spoken en clair, no conversations or voice prints could be used against them.

But of course, it is necessary for the intended victim to actually be where he should be for the assassination to take place and Zebo was beyond furious when they arrived to find the only occupant in the area was Varon's guard who told them the man Roden had not been seen at home the entire day.

With pathetic impotence laughing at Zebo, he and the other men were forced to take cover within the forested area and lie in wait for Roden to return. After three hours, with darkness falling and the night cold setting in to the older bones of the group, Zebo came up with another plan.

'You know where this girl he make love to lives, yes?' The guard nodded and Zebo ordered Varon and his men to remain in the forest – here – while he, Kursk, Gorovitch, Bartok, Davidoff and the guard went

120

further afield towards the girl's residence to see if Roden was camped there for the night. If Roden did return here, Varon was to signal Zebo with just three phone rings. Zebo would then come back to this place. The venture was beginning to resemble an old black & white silent movie where the criminal gang were seen to be utter buffoons while chasing their prey. No-one said this out loud.

This plan was met with minor reservation for it may include the girl and her family becoming involved. A murder of a known assassin would not upset even the British Police – but a Mother and two Daughters – one a child – would definitely set off alarm bells. Zebo nodded, noted the query with justification and walked to his car, followed by his comrades and a now miserable guard who would have much preferred to remain with the only man he knew to be the main Boss – Varon.

Varon and his men sat some considerable distance away from any sight of Roden's house and the nearest neighbour – some quarter of a mile in distance - and a sizeable forage of trees hid them from that neighbour. So well hidden were they, that they felt confident enough to collect wood from the ground and start up a fire. The young men under Varon's wing may easily have been able to sustain themselves in an English forest of a cold night but he, Varon, had old bones and warmth was necessary.

*

Zebo's timing to arrive at the Keeper's Lodge was spot on – not planned of course – but his arrival coincided with the arrival of the Mother, the eldest Daughter - and Roden, who parked his Aston Martin in the parkway just outside the Lodge garden. The home was already lit up so clearly someone was inside and indeed, as Zebo observed, the door was opened by the pretty 12-year old Daughter who hugged her Mother and they all trooped inside.

Zebo checked the faces of the men with him. For Kursk, Gorovitch and Bartok, this was the first time they had seen gun action in years – they had long since passed that particular activity down to their Sons and their soldiers, battling against all potential usurpers to their Crowns, happy to hear the victories were theirs and they would sleep that night and wake up the next morning, heads intact, body still in functioning order.

Zebo ordered Varon's guard to remain outside, to stay in the car and be ready to drive the group away from this house after the job had been completed. Grateful to not be involved in this intended slaughter of children, the guard returned to the car and climbed back in.

The geriatric gangsters moved cautiously towards the house and Davidoff urgently raised his hand to pause them, to crouch down as they reached the edge of the woodland. They did so and a car sped past by. It did not slow, it did not stop. Their assault could continue.

*

Sasha Browne watched Tarra putting the food provisions away as this stranger in their lives – so recent but now, apparently, almost one of the family – was talking to Lainey who screamed with laughter at whatever he was saying to her.

'I'm going back upstairs, Mummy,' shouted Lainey and without waiting for the reply, opened the door and heaved herself up the steep wooden stairs towards the bedrooms. Nate observed there was more than one source of noise above them. Tarra smiled and said, 'Lainey's second slumber party. They each have two a week. Mummy's exhausted.'

Sasha nodded – 'Didn't have slumber parties when I was 12,' she said and the tiredness showed in her face, could be heard in her voice. It was now after nine o'clock and normally, at this time, she would be preparing for her bedtime. Between the raucous goings-on upstairs – and God knows what kind of behaviour between her 22-year old Daughter and her new paramour down here - Sasha didn't feel anything like going to bed. She wavered, watching Nate make three cups of tea and only went into the room when the cups were completed and they were walking into the main lounge.

For Nate, this was the first time he had seen the living arrangements of Tarra's family. He had already heard about the reasons for this social down-sizing and was expecting something along the lines a Dickensian hovel where all were effectively confined to the same room and only bedsheets hung on a clothes line kept their individual privacy intact.

In fact, the room was anything but uncomfortable or undesirable. Most families on an ordinary wage income would be happy as happy people could be living in such a luxurious abode. Admittedly, not much of the 21st century lived here as Tarra had told Nate that the Lodge came already furnished and the furnishing was obligatory to the Lodge at this time. Maybe, by comparison, it would have been difficult, if not impossible, to exchange this furniture for that which they were forced to leave behind in their more grand and opulent former home but there was nothing here in this place that anyone could be ashamed of, thought Nate. It is very well set out and comfortable and who could ask for more?

Well, he thought, Tarra and her Mother for starters. As they entered the lounge, there was almost a look of shame on their faces as they gazed around the area – possibly expecting Nate to look down at his nose upon their great misfortune and who would want such sympathy from a man such as…?

Which was a difficult question to answer as they still really did not know what Nate Roden was apart from wealthy and in open display of it wherever he drove, whoever walked past his home if the gates were open and saw the extraordinary home he apparently had designed and had built. Yes, they would be thinking, wealth lives there – but what is the source of his wealth? Legal, moral, honest?

Sasha sat down, Tarra placed her own cup on the side-table where she was about to sit and Nate the same on the far sofa…

When…

The sight of a total stranger entering your home, especially late at night, is enough to give anyone the screaming abdabs and Sasha was no different under such a circumstance as three men just sauntered into the lounge and were clearly carrying weapons. She screamed.

This alerted Tarra – who joined in the screaming, brief but loud – and before Nate Roden had the chance to sit down he was being thrust aside and backed up towards the two women at gunpoint.

Now the two terrified women clung to each other in fear, whereas Nate Roden put his hands up as if he was familiar to be in the company of a hold-up Agent with a gun. He stared at the three men, knew he didn't know them, then looked down at the weaponry they were holding – quite correctly, he noted so they weren't amateurs. Whether it was bravado or he was just naturally calm under such extreme circumstances no-one knew but it was he who spoke first.

'These men are holding Mini-Uzi sub-machine guns,' he informed everyone in the room. 'They fire 950 rounds a minute, spread over 200 metres. Just a few seconds of a single burst will rip your body apart at a close distance. Tarra, Sasha, whatever you do, do not make any urgent moves or give these men any reason to believe you are a threat to them.'

Warning given. The scenario even settled down a bit which notably gave the three men reason to believe they were now in total control of the situation. One of the men shouted 'We are secure, Patrone.' Albanian, Nate told himself. Gangsters possibly – but what on Earth was this all about?

Another two men entered the room. One young, one much older, early seventies thought Nate and obviously the "Patrone" of the group.

And this gave Nate an idea of who these men were – his personal journey experiences had taken him through Albania and he'd heard of the Shqiptose Mafia. But again, what the hell was this all about?

The "Patrone" took centre position. He, like the other three, held a Mini-Uzi machine gun. The younger man held an automatic in both hands, again in the correct fashion. He remained standing at the back of the group, looking around the room and behind him. These men, regardless of what this was all about, were definitely professionals and Nate made no protests or committed any physical acts of defiance which could easily be misunderstood. To do so would be to be cut down in seconds and there was too much to learn before he acted. He kept his hands in the air to demonstrate his compliance. Sasha noted his lack of fear and drew a conclusion that he must know what this was all about.

Zebo Tulse spoke – bad English and with a thick accent but still understandable.

'So,' he said, 'You are Natty Rodden.' A pause followed and Nate politely corrected the pronunciation of his name without sounding threatening or trying to sound clever. Zebo just stared, drew a small smile and looked at his three comrades, commenting on the man's chutzpah in the face of imminent death and they all nodded in agreement. He moved forward, took out his phone, scrolling down the list. He selected the images he was searching for in his right hand, holding the Uzi in his left. He then slowly leaned over towards Nate and showed him the whole film of Tito Tulse being killed by the Vagabond. Nate, hands still raised above his head, watched the few moments of the fight and grimaced when he saw the death strike. The images ended with the death of Tito. Zebo chose the now familiar freeze frame image of the Vagabond killer and Nate looked at it.

Zebo moved back. 'My Son,' he said. 'Killed. Assassinated.' Pause – and then… 'Killed by you, Natty Rodden.'

Which brought out a minor gasp from Tarra and Sasha. He looked to them and saw the horrified expressions on their faces. He then attended his expression of total confusion on his own face towards Zebo and said, 'That wasn't me. I haven't killed anyone. I don't even look like the man on the phone. I don't even know who you are.'

Pause. Zebo Tulse identified himself and gave the name of his dead Son. Nate stared, in the process of trying to recall both names. Eventually, he shook his head. 'No,' he said.

And for some reason which even he could not explain, Zebo believed him.

Now one of the other men interjected. 'You also kill Edon Bashkim. Two day before.'

Again, Nate protested. Not me, he told them. When did these killings occur, he asked, because I haven't been outside of the UK in weeks.

But the killings had happened nearly a year ago and it had taken them this length of time to learn of the true identity of the assassin who had taken part in the killings of two Sons of important men.

Powerful men. Men of substance. Nate Roden didn't even have to enquire about anything from that moment on – he knew exactly who these men were. But not why they were here, nor why he was being accused of a double murder.

And now there was an intervention of another kind. Kursk was searching the room. 'Where is Davidoff?' he asked, concerned, for the man was as a bodyguard to Zebo while he and his two comrades kept their prey at bay. Zebo turned, equally confused but never taking his Uzi away from the direction of Nate Roden.

He nodded towards Kursk. 'Go find Davidoff.' Kursk left the lounge. Nate added the odds up – now there are just three of them and their Leader still wants to talk.

'You go to Albania,' said the man. Nate nodded. 'Three, maybe four year ago,' he said. 'North. Also Skopie.'

So, there *was* an Albanian connection. This proves it. Gorovitch said so to Zebo in his own language. Nate saw minor confusion on the Leader's face. He raised his hand to Gorovitch – no more interrupting, it conveyed.

Kursk ventured out of the kitchen area and towards the vestibule. Here it was quiet and slightly dark. A light from outside was the rooms only source of clear vision.

'Davidoff?' he asked out loud and fixed his eyes on the far end of the vestibule and saw a pair of men shoes placed under a curtain. 'Davidoff, what you…?' A gloved hand reached out from behind him, it held a blade. A curved blade, like a tiny scimitar, thin, pointed and sharpened on both sides. Whichever way the blade was used, either to stab or slash, the blade would work. Kursk was so set staring at the shoes, he did not even feel the blade slide across the left side of his neck as it sliced open his carotid artery and blood jetted out. He was only aware something not right was happening when he felt the hot blood – *his* hot blood - seeping out from his neck and pouring down his clothes, inside and out. He felt the weakness almost immediately and his legs began to crumble below. His mouth opened and he was about to scream for assistance when the shoes behind the curtain came to life and moved. The curtain was swept away and a man walked into the vestibule, a gun held in his right hand. A large white handkerchief was produced by the killer, still standing behind Kursk and it covered his face so he would not make a noise as he sunk to the floor. Davidoff, the knife killer, whirled him around and Kursk looked up to see the face of the other man standing over him. He expressed a look of shock and surprise. It was his final deliberate act in life.

He slid to the ground and was dead within seconds of being gently laid out by Davidoff. As violent deaths go, this was quiet and would be considered merciful in their home land.

Davidoff looked upward at the owner of the black and highly polished shoes, nodded and left the vestibule.

In the lounge, Nate had carefully moved from his position nearer to Sasha and Tarra and placed himself between them and the men holding Uzi's. Terrified as she was, Tarra was scouring the room to see what could possibly be used as a weapon.

'Why you go to Skopia?' asked Zebo Tulse and now there was doubt in his eyes. Tito, he knew, had never been to Macedonia and if this man was telling the truth, why would he even admit to going to both Albania and Macedonia?

So Nate gave Zebo extensive details on what he was – a gambler, playing cards at casinos and Gaming Palaces - also investing in stocks and shares which took him all over the globe.

Plausible, thought Tarra – a little more than he'd given her but, after all, why would he give her chapter and verse of his life? He didn't barely know her and they weren't exactly picking out names for their babies or choosing flowery curtains to replace the heavy dark blue ones in his home.

Gorovitch stared at Zebo – he was looking like a man who now had doubts. We have flown halfway around the world, he told himself, to find and kill this man and now he is having doubts? Anyone else and Gorovitch would have believed it in an instant – but Zebo???

And as this scenario turned to a tableau, Davidoff entered the room and stood behind Zebo.

Bartok spoke harshly. 'Davidoff,' he snarled, 'you are to stay behind Patrone, to guard him – do not walk from here until you are given leave to…'

And Davidoff replied by putting his automatic up against Zebo's head and ordering the Tulse Patrone to remain still and not to fire upon anybody yet.

Davidoff was stood directly behind Zebo and therefore cut off from the sights of Bartok and Gorovitch so neither could fire on him.

Nate didn't know what was happening but it seemed to be more than mere dissension in the ranks. He was still planning his next move when another man entered the room, strode to its centre and turned towards Zebo who stared at him – a look of total disbelief and shock on his face. Likewise, from Gorovitch and Bartok.

Vanna Bashkim stood tall, dressed in a long black coat, wearing a black Homburg hat. Tall, sturdy, old yes, but clearly a man of power, a man of substance – and now, a man who was in complete control of the situation that just a few moments ago had been occupied by the Patrone.

Gorovitch and Bartok stated at the transformation of the man they had seen a short while ago. Then, defeated, pathetic, weak, small even. Now, tall and vibrant, a leader – stronger even than Zebo. How did this transformation take place? *When* did this transformation take place? How could man who had wept in front of other men, suddenly become a man who exuded power, for even Bartok and Gorovitch could sense it. Vanna Bashkim was a man of substance and *he was here*… How? Why?

It suddenly came to Bartok. That day, when Zebo and the comrades had visited Bashkim in his own home and he had fallen to the floor in despair seemingly over the death of his Son, the whole thing was nothing but a performance – put on for the benefit of Zebo, Bartok, Gorovitch and Kursk. A masquerade. They had been faked into believing Bashkim was a beaten man, simply waiting his time out to die and pass on the rule to one of his remaining Sons.

But why?

And Davidoff – what was his part in this performance – for now he was no longer the reluctant soldier serving another army's General. Now he was a man who looked as determined as Vanna Bashkim himself – and Bartok suddenly realised Davidoff had been planted on them. To work with Zebo and his comrades – but also to report back to Bashkim every day – inform him of all their progress and their next actions. A walking talking tracking device. And Davidoff had told his Leader they were coming to the UK, when and where they would be headed.

And again, he asked himself – why?

Out of nowhere and completely unexpected, the answer came from Nate Roden.

'Bashkim?' he said out loud.

They all stared at him – a slow turning of heads – and in the doing so, the deathly threats were diffused somewhat. Recognition of Vanna Bashkim must have had relevance. If this Englishman, Roden, had nothing to do with the murders of Tito Tulse and Edon Bashkim, how on Earth would he even know Vanna Bashkim?

Vanna Bashkim slowly and fully turned his own body to engage with Nate Roden. As he did so, Davidoff pressed his automatic into the back of Zebo's head, grabbing him by the collar of his coat as he did so. The movement told Bartok and Gorovitch that even the minutest movement, wrongly interpreted, would result in the immediate death of Zebo Tulse.

Vanna smiled. 'So, Englishman,' he said, in English better spoken than that which came from Zebo Tulse, 'You recognize me. You remember me. I am honoured. But then, such a battle between us.'

Battle? So, Sasha thought. This Nate Roden, who wishes to score with my Daughter, *IS* a gangster after all.

'Three, three and half years ago,' responded Nate Roden and now his voice had changed, to something more aggressive. 'The Apollonia Casino, The FlaminGo Casino in Skopia first, then The Grand and Royal Eagle Casinos in Tirana. The Marathon Games. Twenty games in total – ten men started – two men at the end. You… and me.'

'And you win against me,' said Vanna, still smiling. 'Ten…. How you say in your money…?'

'Million,' said Nate Roden. 'Ten million. Quid. Ten… million… quid.'

Suddenly, for Sasha and Tarra, answers were now forthcoming. Not much in the way of clarity yet but answers. Nate – and this… Bash… chappie… had played a game of cards…

…and Nate had won.

And this card game is what this outrage is all about?

Another pause followed and then Vanna said, 'You cheat me.'

At which, Nate protested, now confident enough to drop his hands.

'The hell I did. Cheat? You drew the final hand and made a Call. The wrong Call. You screwed up, Bashkim. I won fair and square. The Courier told you that the same night you lodged a protest to the Gaming Federation. They all told you. They even showed the CCTV film where you made the Call. You lost, buddy. I won that £10,000,000 true.'

And Bashkim merely smiled. He raised his own gun.

At which point, Sasha decided to put her ten pence worth in.

'Are you people telling us that this… bloody gun thing is happening… because of a game of cards?'

Zebo responded first. 'He kill my Son…'

And Nate yelled back. 'I didn't kill your bloody Son. I never even met him. Look at your damn phone. Does that killer even look like me?'

And Vanna Bashkim then dropped the bomb. He struck at his chest with his hand – gun still in evidence. *'I KILL YOU SON, ZEBO! I – VANNA BASHKIM – THE MAN YOU ALL THINK IS OLD AND DEAD WAITING TO TAKE HIS FINAL BREATH! I KILL YOU SON!'*

The silence which followed was enough for everyone to take stock of the situation in a different light. Clearly something else had occurred here for the facial expressions on Zebo Tulse and the two men with Uzi's was of complete shock.

Vanna stood back – breathing out and loud – and he looked up, staring Zebo dead in the face.

'YOU… treat me as a man of no account – a small man of little substance, to be ridiculed – *IN FRONT OF YOU OTHER MEN! ME…'*

And now he stepped forward, his gun pushed into Zebo's face. His rage was palpable though now fairly restrained given the level of his anger.

'I AM WARRIOR,' he screamed. *'I… UNLIKE YOU… FIGHT IN THE BATTLE WE HAVE… MANY YEAR I FIGHT WHILE YOU… HIDE… BEHIND YOU FATHER APRON STRINGS. I KILL… WITH MY BARE HAND… WITH GUN AND KNIFE…. WITH BOMB… I KILL MEN WHO ARE ALSO WARRIOR… AND YOU COWER BEHIND THAT BASTARD VARON. HIM… I RESPECT. HE IS A WARRIOR ALSO… BUT YOU… YOU JUST LAUGH AT ME LIKE I AM NOTHING!!!'*

He backed away and Zebo stared at him, wide-eyed, fearing this newly found power coming from a man who, just a short time ago, was considered to be soon gone from this world. It was a hard realisation for Zebo, Gorovitch and Bartok to take in.

And Gorovitch then made a calamitous error of judgement.

'Kursk,' he blurted out, 'where is…?' – and Vanna swung at him with his left hand. At first, there seemed to be little contact made and Gorovitch appeared not be harmed. At first.

Sasha screamed.

The white shirt worn by Gorovitch had turned deep red and the red was spreading. He stared ahead, now acknowledging the pain and the loss of blood which was now seeping out from his throat. The thin, scimitar-shaped blade used on the now dead Kursk had made its mark a second time. This time, the throat slash wound was more visible and the blood poured out. He stretched his hand towards Zebo as if just the man's physical presence would be enough to stem the blood-flow.

It wasn't and Oska Gorovitch collapsed to the floor, joining Marku Kursk in death within seconds.

And this told the story – or a part of it. Everybody saw what happened and Zebo and Bartok now knew the fate which had taken Kursk. Yes, Zebo thought, Vanna was always the expert with the blade. He even fashioned his own. All kinds of blades, he had seen this particular blade in action before. Vanna always struck at the most vulnerable parts of the opponent's bodies. Always the neck and throat. Sometimes he'd stab his opponent in the eyes.

Again, the scene calmed down. Vanna took control of his rage and carried on his converse as though had happened in between the rages. He turned his ahead, constantly, to address everybody in the room.

'My Son,' he said, 'he plot against me. He plot… with Tito Tulse. Yes, my old friend, Zebo. My Son, you Son. They plot together. Why? To remove us. We, who for year after year, keep our Families safe and secure from all outsider, they decide we are too old to be allowed to continue. We are too soft, I hear him say, "My Father," he say, "is ready for grave." And you Son say "Yes, I agree."

He walked up to Zebo and stood almost nose-to-nose – again, he jabbed at his chest. 'I kill my Endo – I order the death on you Son. A man – no name, a mercenary perhaps – he know where you Son will be at Mnsk for I tell him so. I wait for this day. I send this man in. You phone image…' He snatched the phone out of Zebo's hand and showed it to everybody in the room and smiled broadly. 'This image… is made by the boy, Rado… he film this fight… as I instruct him to. This boy Rado…,' And here he smiled again, now proudly beating at his chest, '…is my *Grandson!!!* He do this thing for me. I have good Grandson.'

Another pause and Vanna took out a small hip-flask and swigged something from it.

Zebo re-joined the discourse – a man who now looked and sounded terrified and was hoping Varon and his men were tired of waiting at this man Roden's home and had decided to come here to check out the lie of the land. He hoped.

'But our search for this man, Roden,' he spoke with a trembling in his voice. Fear, confusion. 'His name and whereabouts were given to us by the Agent who hire the man who assassinate my Tito.'

And Vanna screamed with laughter. Again, he jabbed at his chest. '*I…*' he screamed, '*I AM THE AGENT WHO SEND YOU TO THIS COUNTRY. EVERYTHING YOU DO, ZEBO, MY… OLD… FRIEND… IS DIRECTED BY ME.*'

And Zebo slowly sunk into his body. He had been directed from moment one in this venture to avenge his Son's death – and directed by a man whom he'd considered to be less than nothing – not just by him but by other smaller Captains of the Shqiptose Mafia. Out-manoeuvred, out-played, out-fought – and this plan was constructed by a clever person who had engineered everybody else's hands and directions to his own bidding.

Nate decided to come back. 'It seems like you've gone to a lot of effort to get to me and your friend there.'

Vanna turned back to him. 'Revenge, is always worth effort if you wish to win and continue to rise above you fellow man. I lose ten… ten… how you say?'

'Ten million,' said Nate, Sasha and Tarra in chorus – and then Tarra added 'Quid' to emphasis the point…

'Ah, replied Vanna. 'Yes. Million. I cannot take that back to Albania with me – but I can tell my people the man who cheat me is now dead – *AT MY HAND!!!* And also too, the man who think he own Albania.' He pointed the scimitar blade at Zebo and smiled.

'I don't understand why you didn't kill this man in your own country,' said Nate. 'Why bring him all the way here?' He moved slightly to his left. There was an object there he wanted to be within grabbing distance if all this really did kick off. He, Sasha and Tarra were stood behind the larger of the two sofas which should offer them a little protection in the event of a bullet-fest kicking off.

Vanna replied to Nate's comment.

'You are correct, Englishman Natty Rodden,' Nate didn't bother correcting anyone this time. Even that gesture might spark a tirade. He wanted things to be as calm as possible. 'But you understand, when you are General in Shqiptose Mafia, you are protected by many dangerous warrior soldiers. Not easy for to assassinate – especially for man who do not leave his home palace many time. I think of plan to make him angry enough to leave his home and even leave country which Zebo Tulse never do before. He need reason to keep his Honour for he is *"GENERAL TULSE"* – Head of Mafia in Albania.'

He then moved towards Zebo who seemed to be visibly shrinking in front of everyone in the room. 'And to come to this benighted country without people knowing he has left Albania – he must have Passport in different name. Different identity. You understand, Englishman?'

Nate added the figures up. 'Different name and identity, means no-one at home knows he's come here. Officially, he hasn't even left Albania. Kill him here – and his Lieutenants – nobody at home knows he's dead. Or who killed him.'

Vanna laughed. 'Is good plan – yes? I kill him to strengthen my own position at home – I earn respect from other Warriors. I kill you because you humiliate me in card game – I earn respect from other Warriors. I win.'

Moving away from Nate, he addressed Zebo once again.

'And I know what you think – you friend Varon – you think he come to rescue you ass like he do so many time – no, old friend Zebo. Not this time. You friend Varon – he is dead. Killed by MY people – another part of *MY* plan.' Pause. Silence. Vanna raised his own gun to Zebo's head and Davidoff moved a step back. 'Time to die,' he said.

The interruption came from a completely different direction which took everybody by surprise. Even Nate.

The white door leading to the upstairs bedrooms opened and Lainey pranced into the room…

'Mummy, can we stay up till…?'

Sasha screamed at Lainey. The door had opened across the aim of Bartok's Uzi. He had held back, thus far, in restraint, up till now, not knowing exactly what to do. This was true for everybody carrying guns in the small confines of the lounge for if just one bullet was fired a hail of bullets would flow and everything would have been hit, ripped apart, including the fleshpot humans.

Bartok's reaction was very much an on-the-spot move and he aimed his Uzi at the door. Nate had no choice but to act.

He ripped a sturdy and heavy-looking table lamp out of its plug socket and hurled it at the side of Bartok's head, catching him on the left temple. It was enough, at any rate, to deflect his aim and only the base of the door was struck by a few seconds worth of rapid magazine firing from the Uzi.

Sasha and Tarra screamed and Bartok collapsed against the door slamming it shut. Lainey – not knowing what the hell was going on downstairs – at least had the savvy to high-tail it back upstairs and out of the way.

And that's when the shooting battle kicked off.

Davidoff had taken his gun away from Zebo for fear of hitting his own Patrone inadvertently. Instead, he took aim at Nate though not wanting to kill him as it was Vanna's specific instructions to him that while he had carte blanche to kill anyone else, Zebo and Nate were to be his kills and no-one else's.

Bartok's Uzi was still in firing mode though he was now only semi-conscious. His finger was pressed against the trigger.

Davidoff's aim at Nate was too high and Nate had also ducked down behind the sofa. His mind was racing to come up with another projectile to use against the enemy when he saw Tarra moving across the carpeted floor like a snake. She reached the far end of the room and dragged out from under a small table a large carton containing a brown liquid. She took its cap off and stood as Davidoff made his way to get a better aim at Nate.

Because of the distraction, Vanna had failed to fire directly at Zebo – and Zebo swiftly regained his ground and leapt at Vanna. It was enough for him to grasp Vanna's wrist and prevent him from firing the gun at him again but it was still fired twice more.

Davidoff stood, victoriously, over the prone Nate and aimed his gun – and was then covered in whatever substance was contained in the carton Tarra was holding. The substance covered his head, in his eyes, inside his mouth and upper half of his body and he screaming when the oil burned into his eyes.

Nate got to his feet and saw the two aged Mafia men battling against each other without actually landing any telling blows. He dived over the arms of the sofa and armchair, striking both men with open palms and the blows were enough to send them crashing to the floor where they continued their writhing and screaming and lashing out.

And now it was Davidoff who was screaming. Nate turned and saw the man's head was on fire.

When the Browne family moved into the Lodge, one of the first things which became apparent was how the house was warmed by an actual fire – not radiators – and the source of house lighting did not come from the electric lights on the ceiling but from oil lamps placed around the room. There were at least five.

Sasha had followed up on Tarra's actions – she had grabbed a Zhen Yu Mayflower oil lamp which was lit and active and had hurled it at Davidoff. The glass base had smashed against the wall and the fire from its wick had landed on top of Davidoff's head. The flame joined the oil Tarra had thrown on him and engulfed him around his face, the back of his head and his shoulders. He screamed and in the process of doing so, lost grip of his gun.

Nate snatched it up just as Bartok was regaining his senses. As the Uzi was lifted, Nate fired once into the man's forehead and Dervishi Bartok joined his two comrades in death.

But now there was another problem, for Davidoff, ablaze now, was staggering about the lounge and setting anything flammable alight. The curtains and the two sofas, both recipients of the spilt oil, were now raging fires and this presented Sasha, Tarra and Nate with a problem because their only route was cut off either by fire or by the two old men lashing out at each other with unquenchable hatred.

Zebo's Uzi was within grabbing distance on the floor where the fire was spreading and Nate snatched it up. He turned to the window which was old and held in check by criss-cross metal bars in diamond form. He fired at the whole window frame and emptied the clip into it. Then he picked up a small cabinet and charged at the window, smashing into it five times before it was removed from its frame. A few more strikes and the whole window, plus frame, was sent crashing onto the garden beyond.

The fire had taken a real grip of the room now – much of it being made from wood so it had plenty of opportunity to unleash its fiery hell on everything which could burn.

Nate dragged Tarra to her feet, grabbed her under the legs and her arms and hurled her out of the room. She landed on top of the smashed windows on the other side.

He moved towards Sasha who was screaming for Lainey.

Nate grabbed hold of Sasha and told her he would bring Lainey down, one way or the other.

'There are five other girls up there,' Sasha screamed, now choking from the oily smoke billowing around the room.

He moved her to the frameless window and hoisted her up and out, to be caught by Tarra.

He pushed the blazing sofa away so the fire was now concentrated on the other side of the room. Bartok's body was leaning against the door and Nate had to drag him away.

Unbelievably, in spite of the hell raging all around them, Zebo and Vanna were still grasping at each other. The deaths of others and the fire were to be ignored as the two enemies grappled for supremacy.

The fire had now snaked its way up to the ceiling – helped by the dry wooden walls – and the ceiling itself was no barrier to it spreading across the room. Parts of the ceiling were erupting and some of it crashed on top of Nate. Hurt, in pain, burned, he moved on.

He yanked open the door and ran up the stairs – and damn, they were steep. He reached the landing and saw it had a long corridor and rooms were situated on both sides.

'*LAINEY*,' he screamed, and screaming came right back at him. 'We're over here,' shouted the dulcet tones of the very vocal Lainey and Nate rushed to where she and her fellow slumber-ites were ensconced.

His initial plan was to take the six girls back down the stairs, to keep to the side wall which had not been set on fire and then throw them through the window. That idea came to a stop when he saw the fire had broken through the door and was now making its way up the steep stairs.

Keeping his head – he thought laterally. Lainey came out of the room she and her friends were hiding in. 'What the hell is happening, Nate…?' she asked before seeing the smoke billowing up the towards the landing. 'Oh shite,' she said and deferred to Nate.

'Bathroom?' he asked and she pointed. 'Bucket,' he shouted, 'any kind of container. *NOW!*

Nate went to the bath and the sink, rammed the plugs into their respective plug-holes and turned all the taps on full. Then he went to the main bedroom. The girls followed him. He picked up a medium-sized cabinet and performed the same task on the bedroom window he had done on the lounge window. The window frame was long – maybe about six feet in length, four feet in height – and he stabbed at the window until it, like its counterpart in the lounge, was removed from the frame and it toppled out and down into the garden below. He swept the duvet covering the double sized mattress and was about to drag the mattress off the bed when he heard Lainey scream.

He rushed to where she was standing – a mop mucket in her hand – and saw the fire was now on the landing carpet and making its way up the walls. He ran into the bathroom where the plunging waterfalls of the bath and sink were doing what he wanted – which was to cover the floor. He used Lainey's mop bucket, scooped a whole bucketful and swept it across the wooden floor which partially doused the flames and dampened the remaining carpet. He repeated the act and threw the water around the walls. Then he went as far as the edge of the stairs and spread a bucketful of water down to the door which was now almost off its hinges.

He grabbed Lainey and they rushed back to Sasha's bedroom. He took the mattress off the bed and hurled it out of the window and saw, with great relief, neighbours and friends down below who had seen or heard the fracas coming from the Lodge and had performed their neighbourly duties to come and see if assistance was required.

Was it ever?

The neighbours had gleaned Nate's plan and they took corners and sides of the mattress and held it like a safety net. Nate grabbed Libbi first and ordered her to keep her body rigid and her arms crossed across her chest which she did and he picked her up. Standing on the ledge of the window sill, he then threw the rigid 12-year old girl out and she landed directly on top of the suspended mattress. She bounced off it – and fortuitously was caught by her own Father. He held onto her for dear life and they ran from the Lodge which was now almost engulfed in flames. Once safe with her Mother, Father ran back to the mattress-holding saviours.

Ellee, Evie, Rubee, Olyvia and new Slumber-ite, Phillipa Beddoes, all did as was instructed by this man who had saved Phillipa before, they had all heard about it, and then saved Tarra from Billy Telling's nonsense. He was in charge, he had just saved Libbi. Being thrown from the bedroom onto a mattress is no biggie they all said and besides, it looked like fun.

All five girls were caught by the mattress saviours below – and to his surprise, Nate saw one of the neighbours holding the mattress was Billy Telling. William Telling was among the group pumping water from an 18th century water-pump water-well into buckets and throwing them at the Lodge. Futile effort, the fire had now taken over most of the Lodge but they still endeavoured to bring the fire down before the Fire Engines arrived.

The last girl to leave – at her own insistence – was Lainey. She had even bravely consoled her frightened friends, telling them this man was a hero and he could do almost anything. What Tarra had been telling her was anybody's guess but her words of comfort had worked for none of them panicked.

But Lainey was panicking now. After the last girl but her had been thrown out, a man crashed into the room and she saw he was completely on fire. She screamed.

Vanna Bashkim was literally covered in flames. Not volcanic erupting flames but the kind which just about cover an area which has been coated with some kind of ointment which allows the fire to burn but not to actually make a burning impact. Stunt co-ordinators use a lotion in films to give the impression a person is on fire without that particular stunt-person actually being set alight. It was that impression now that Nate had looking at Vanna. Not completely covered though as his face was charred and flames licked at what flesh was left available. Lainey screamed again.

Under normal fighting conditions, Nate would have let fly with something like a Roundhouse kick, or even a flying kick into the face – but here, he daren't allow himself to come into any kind of contact with Vanna for fear of the flames transferring from one body to another. He opted for the old reliable methods instead. Throwing heavy objects.

Yet another sturdy light lamp was found and set next to Sasha's bed. Nate ripped it out from its plug socket and threw it at Vanna's face. Vanna clearly felt the effect of the heavy lamp crashing into him for he screamed out loud, proving the fire had not dulled his nervous system yet. Nate lifted the base of the bed and used it to barricade Vanna against the doorway which, Nate noticed, was also on fire. Vanna screamed.

He ran to Lainey and ordered her to adopt the prone and rigid position, 'just like your friends did,' and she did so without pause. He scooped her up and screamed *'SHE'S COMING OUT'* to whomever was directly below and he went to the window and dropped her out.

It was Billy who caught her and in one single move, whirled around on his feet and passed her into the arms of Sasha who then ran away from the burning building.

Nate turned to see the bed base was now also on fire. He pushed up against the base of the bed, pinning it against Vanna. He now prepared to perform a dive out of the window and hoped someone below was still holding the mattress up for him to land on.

But...

The base of the bed was sent back smashing at him and Vanna stood, upright, his arm stretched outward, an accusing finger pointed directly at Nate.

'YOU CHEATED ME…' he screamed and Nate had never heard a sound like it. Guttural and hoarse, a voice in flames and sounding as if it came from the very depths of Hell.

And as he stood there in accusing fury, the bedroom floor suddenly caved in – or downwards – and Vanna Bashkim screamed all the way down to his own personal Hell for Nate could see the fire in the rooms below was raging out of control.

An explosion prevented Nate from executing his next move – jumping out of the window.

The explosion caught him badly about the body and face and he fell back – the fire now creeping up to the window frame and was raging too much for him to take the risk of trying to dive through it.

More of the bedroom floor gave way which aided the fire below to increase in size and his options were limited. Practically the whole bedroom was now ablaze – and if the fire had made it this far then the other bedrooms were also on fire.

He heard his name being called from outside and knew Tarra was screaming for him to jump. With just a few feet between him and the gaping fire-strewn hole in the bedroom floor he had but one single option left.

So far, the fire had taken its rage out on the door, the floor and the walls – but the ceiling was not yet touched. He leapt from where he was pinioned and grabbed the faux chandelier, hoping it would take his weight and allow him to swing across the blazing hole and land on the other side of the bedroom where there was at least more purchase room to stand on.

Well, it did – to a point – he landed on enough floor to stand on but the chandelier came crashing out from its ceiling fixture and it too fell down into the fire below.

The door was too engulfed in flames to push away but then he saw the wires hanging out of the ceiling which had held the chandelier which had kept it secured in place in the apparatus above the ceiling and in the Lodge loft. Desperate now – he was out of time and space – he jumped, caught the wiring and it held his weight. He then swung and kicked upwards on the remaining ceiling which was falling around him.

Outside, the Police had arrived. Three cars – not, as it turned out, for this emergency but for another incident further down the road. This one, apparently, took precedence.

Twelve Police Officers scrambled out of their cars and ran to where the brave neighbours were still trying to put the fire out by the use of the water pump and buckets. They were ordered to abandon their courageous attempt and to abandon the area before…

…too late. The Lodge suddenly erupted. The house walls and roof were blown out by a huge explosion and large fragments of stone and wood, all on fire, crashed down on everybody within a twenty-yard radius. Police Officers and neighbours all rushed to rescue those who had fallen and weren't getting back to their feet under their own steam and they carried those wounded people to a safer place.

Another Police Officer had called the Fire Service though at least ten calls had already been made. This call, coming from an Officer attending the emergency, may have generated more urgency.

More explosions followed and Sasha confirmed to one Officer there were combustible tanks inside the building. The entire ground troops were now well away from the emergency area and after ten minutes, sirens could be heard. A Fire Engine from one direction, an Ambulance from another.

More Emergency vehicles approached as the night wore on. All the neighbours were moved from their homes as they were all surrounded by forestry and the fire had reached the trees and now they were also alight. After a relatively dry period, the trees were prime for a burning.

Sasha watched, helplessly, as her home crashed to the ground and burned into the night.

C H A P T E R   2 2
THE INCIDENT ROOM

The danger zone was widened from the burning house where the Fire Services were still active in putting the fire out – both at the house and the surrounding woodland. They would be there for quite a long time to come. The Ambulances dealt with those who had received any kind of burns – not many and, thankfully, no-one seriously harmed.

Blessedly, none of those innocents who had actually been in the house had been harmed from the terrifying inferno though they were still all packed off to Ipswich General Hospital for safety sake. Smoke inhalation was a common factor in such incidents and let's not be too blasé about how lucky everybody was.

An Incident Room was set up by the Police for the sake of swift expediency. An empty Community Hall, well away from where any incumbent patients were lying in bed, was used so as not to disturb those who were asleep.

Sasha was initially kept away from everybody else as questions about how the fire was started were asked. When she mentioned the house had been invaded by men with guns, the concern suddenly took a different turn. The Police had already been called out to attend a shooting incident – but not at this address. Somewhere else. 'Ever heard of Haydock's Barn?' asked one Officer and Tarra all but fainted.

Sasha then gave the Officers as much information as she had been able to understand from the intruders from their thick middle-European accents. She ran through it exactly as it had taken place. She, Tarra and this man named Nate Roden – Tarra's friend – had come home, and within minutes they were all subjected to the invasion by the five men, all armed with guns, then a sixth man with a gun and a knife. A fight broke out, bullets were fired, people were killed and they got out of the house. She and Tarra were thrown out of the house by the man Roden who then went upstairs to rescue the six children. Here, she looked over to the other room which had a window in a door separating her from her Daughters and she could see where Tarra and Lainey were now placed. Tarra was sat upright – staring ahead, a blank expression on her face and tears still rolling down her cheeks mourning the loss of Nate for there was no way he could have survived those explosions. The men with guns were dead for sure and Nate had sacrificed his life to save the children – and Lainey, now lying asleep on her lap - had been one of them. A Female Police Officer was in the room with them and sitting near Tarra. She was talking and Tarra was either nodding or shaking her head but not speaking – speaking was impossible.

Sasha continued her statement. She observed there was a dispute between two of the foreign men and it as they who started the fight. Nate had protected her and Tarra – and it may have been her and Tarra who possibly ignited the fire by her throwing the oil lamp at one of the men who had fired at Nate followed by her daughter throwing a carton of oil meant for the lamps.

Nate had thrown her and Tarra out through the broken window in the lounge and then went up to the bedrooms to try and rescue the children – which he did – she saw him throwing them out of the bedroom after he had thrown out the mattress to give them a soft landing.

'The explosions must have killed him – and them, those other men,' she said. 'The whole place went up like tinder-wood. Never had a chance – poor sod.' And she broke down in tears for now, having spoken those words out loud, she realised how close she had come to losing both her Daughters.

The question of how Mister Roden was involved in the first place was less easy for her to answer and for this, she called upon Tarra to assist. Tarra rested Lainey on the bench, covered her with her coat and joined her Mother in the Incident Room.

In the easiest of terms, Tarra explained how one of the foreigners had a big resentment against one of the other foreigners and had used Nate as a reason to get the man into this country because, for some reason, he couldn't do the killing job in their own country. Oh yes, she added, two Sons of two powerful men had been assassinated – possibly *their* Sons – and this appeared to be the reason why there was dispute between the two men. It all happened very fast and it was hard to understand all their converse because of their accents.

Sasha then included the matter of Nate's gambling experiences and how he had taken ten million quid, fairly won, from one of the men and this was another reason for the man's angry tirade.

As this statement was being spoken and written out by the Investigating Officer, Sasha had noted the entry of a man in plain clothes who had entered the Incident Room. He sat quietly, did not speak with any of the Officers in the room and they did not enquire about his being there.

At the end of the questions and answers session, the plain clothes man stood and approached the desk, picked up the statement sheet and studied it. He smiled when he finished it and handed it back to the Officer who had taken the statement.

'Nate Roden,' said the man, still smiling, and he left the room.

The Officer then took the statement, read the name again and said 'Ah.'

C H A P T E R 2 3
POST MORTEM

The fire, the fighting, the killings, the activities which had involved the Children from The Heath had brought the area into media focus on a scale nobody living there had ever seen before. That no innocent had died was a blessing – not enough of Nate Roden was known by them to know for sure if he was an innocent or not – but they soon learned he had saved the lives of all the people who mattered when the shooting started and the fire was destroying all around him so much benefit of the doubt was given to him.

In the first week which followed the incident and the locals now getting used to seeing tv cameras and journalists, foreign and domestic, trawling around the area seeking personal stories from anyone who was involved in the whole she-bang.

Neighbours rally when one of their own are in deep trouble and the scandal surrounding the Browne Family, courtesy of low-life Daddy Edmund Brown, was no longer a talking point. Sasha - a once discarded neighbour who had lost her own home through her Husband's actions and now a second home because of something even more frightening, was now to be cared for by everybody concerned.

And it was the Beddoes Family who rallied to Sasha's aid first. They were affluent and lived in a very spacious abode, part of which was now vacated as elder daughter, Patrice, was now living closer to the Capital because of her work – therefore, a spare bedroom – designed for a person of such an age – was passed onto the grieving Tarra. Patrice personally brought her there, sat her on the bed and both women cried for a long time as Tarra related to Patrice her brief love affair with Nate and Patrice did what all best friends do, gave her the solace of a shoulder and, when needed, silence, for sometimes mere words of consolation cannot assuage the grief.

Sasha was still in the state of trauma because she could not rid her mind of what could have happened if things had turned out the other way. Not just her home – that was just stone, wood and mortar – but the near possible deaths of her Daughters as well. It was left to Annaliza to hold her tight and instil the reality – Tarra, Lainey, were *NOT* dead – they were alive and living in this very house, fully recovered from their hell and handling it very well. Sasha nodded, she knew, she saw them, it was all alright – but those damn thoughts just kept assailing at her and it brought her down.

Annaliza knew nothing but time and reality would help Sasha and that's what she gave her. She knew if this thing had happened to her and her Daughters, she would be falling apart as well.

Upstairs, Phillipa had held onto Lainey for as long as her strength could last. It is amazing how quickly children assimilate the worst things in life which are thrown at them and these two girls were no different. When they were joined by Libbi, Evie, Olyvia and Ellee, they had the slumber party to end all slumber parties and no parent within earshot objected. Bearing in mind that four of the most immediate neighbours were the parents of the girls this man Roden had saved, their noise was as welcome as a light rain in the throes of a long drought.

It was, therefore, wholly appropriate that Patrice should be the one to run into her home one day, laughing, crying, almost screaming, passing by both Sasha and Annaliza who were taken completely by surprise at this loud, very unlike Patrice, intrusion, and then watch her flying up the stairs to get to Tarra who was lying on the bed, not asleep, but blankly staring at the walls just a few days after the Browne's had been invited to stay at chez Beddoes and all but dived on top of her.

This extraordinary behaviour – extraordinary because it had come from Patrice who was not given to such overly demonstrative emotion – was followed by Tarra screaming and the two of them rushing down the stairs and out of the house.

Sasha and Annaliza, confused, followed them and saw three Police cars parked in the street. One of the cars was an undercover vehicle, only becoming a Police vehicle when its siren and blue lights flashed on and off. Standing next to this car was a woman Police Officer who wore a different kind of uniform to those others who stood around her.

'Oh,' said Annaliza – 'I know who she is. Elizabeth Keene. She's the Deputy Chief Constable for Suffolk County Police. She sometimes sits in on local Council meetings discussing troubles around Ipswich and surrounding areas. Nice lady – always listens to our concerns.'

Tarra and this Keene woman spoke to each other for a few moments and then Tarra was screaming again and wrapped her arms around Patrice's shoulders. Both girls were now screaming and crying – but, apparently, with joy for their smiles were broad and thrilling.

Tarra saw her Mother standing in the doorway and she broke away from Patrice, running up the garden path to where her Mother was standing. She was sobbing – but laughing at the same time. Sasha stood, confused.

'He's alive, Mummy. He's alive. He's… alive… he's ali…' And now her happiness gave way to overwhelming emotion and she broke down in tears. Only Sasha's physical strength kept her standing upright. 'He's alive, Mummy. Nate's alive,' Tarra finally gave out.

A smiling Deputy Chief Constable joined them and said, 'Can we go inside? I have something to tell you all.'

*

DEPUTY CHIEF CONSTABLE ELIZABETH KEENE

'So – all the stories he gave me – travelling about the world, that training he went through at the monastery, the gambling – are all true?'

DCC Keene smiled. The incredulity demonstrated by young Tarra Browne amused her for she had heard the same disbelief from other people who had come into contact with Mister Nate Roden – real name by the way – and had remained in a state of disbelief when they learned what sounded like fanciful stories were, in fact, the truth.

DCC Keene had been warmly welcomed into the Beddoes home – first by Mister Beddoes who had arrived home from his work just a few minutes after the Police entourage had arrived. As her being here was a matter for the Browne's and the Beddoes' families, she was brought inside to see the smiling faces of Phillipa and Lainey who were both introduced to her by their respective Mothers and DCC Keene realised that these two upstanding young ladies had been directly involved in the fire and shooting fracas. She congratulated the two girls on their adventure and their courage in going through such a traumatic business and to still come out of it, smiling.

And so to business of a more adult version. Lainey and Philippa went upstairs while all the adults, and this included Tarra and Patrice, sat down in the large lounge and listened to DCC Keene bring them up to date, informally as it were, before the whole story would be read by the nation in all the national newspapers.

To begin with, the bodies eventually found by the Fire Service were later identified by…

…well, guess who?

Six bodies had been found – five inside the house and one lying in the garden glasshouse about twenty yards up the path. The five bodies in the house had been so badly burned, there was no way to identify them. The later forensics investigation could find no paperwork on them, no driving licenses, to show who these men were. What they did find were a number of shooting weapons which had had their serial numbers filed off – and now destroyed by the fire so no way of even identifying their history neither.

Their clothes were so badly burned, scorched, there were no labels to indicate if they were bought here or abroad.

As far as the five men were concerned, the investigating team came up empty. If there was another cause of death beyond the fire, the initial autopsy drew a blank.

The sixth man, the man found in the smashed-out glasshouse, though seriously burned, had died in a way which could be identified.

This man had a gash across the left side of his neck and across the carotid artery. The gash was deep and could only have been made by a very thin but sharp blade. The blood which had soaked into his clothes and upper body indicated he had died from serious blood loss and the Pathologist estimated more than three-quarters of the body had been exsanguinated. The fire had certainly caught up with him and the prevailing theory was the man had been near the vestibule area of the house when the big explosion had erupted and it had swept his body up in the blast and carried him out through the doors and up to where the glasshouse had been built. Every single pane of glass had been smashed in and much of the framework had been destroyed in the impact the man must have made when he crashed into its structure. Only the strength of the structure had kept it from being completely obliterated.

It took the Fire Service a long night and most of the following day to get the fire at the house and the surrounding forestry under control, making absolutely certain all the trees had been thoroughly soaked, preventing any other stray flames from re-igniting the fire.

As the Fire Control people sifted through the forest to make absolutely certain all fire danger was kept at bay, they found the seriously wounded Mister Nate Roden lying beneath a tall tree, unconscious, burned, wounded by both flame and bullets. At least from him, as he regained consciousness, they were able to get a brief sense of what had transpired at the house. An Ambulance was brought to The Heath and Mister Roden was transported away. By the time he left, a sizeable and plausible picture had become quite clear. His testimony even answered the second mystery of the night – the identities of six other men in another part of the forest who had been bludgeoned then shot to death. It was their early discovery, made by a man walking his dogs, which had brought the first wave of Police to the area to begin with – only stopping when they saw the Browne Lodge on fire. Mister Roden, from his hospital bed, explained how he'd made his way into the Lodge's attic when the first big explosion erupted and the roof was split asunder. He was blown out of the Lodge loft and crashed onto the back garden. With the Lodge still exploding he leapt over the garden fence and ran out of the area. He'd reached the tree and suddenly, unconsciousness overwhelmed him. Now conscious in the Ipswich General Hospital, and of sound mind, he was able to give the Police enough information to work with and Mrs Browne – who smiled at the hand gesture offered by DCC Keene – gave them the rest of the story.

Nate Roden gave the Police as near a complete story as was possible as to who the men were and why they were in the UK – what their direct purpose was and how one of the gangsters had planned the enterprise which would bring about his death and the elimination of the said gangster's enemies.

This information was immediately acted upon and sent out on a wide basis. Eventually, from no less a communication sent to MI6, from the Albanian Government confirming the identities of the men and what their status was relating to the Shqiptose Mafia Cartel. As far as the private conversation between two high ranking Counter-Espionage Operatives was concerned, the general feeling from the Albanian side was – "No loss."

'So this story Nate gave us – the Marathon Card Game – in Albania and… I forget the other country…' This from Tarra.

'Macedonia,' her Mother filled in.

'…was all true? He really did win ten million quid?'

DCC Keene smiled. 'All true,' she said. 'And Mister Roden's victory inadvertently prevented a war between one branch of the Albanian Cartel and another branch. This… Bashkim… was angry enough to go to war against his fellow Cartel members because he felt they had not shown him enough respect. He planned a war – but for that he needed money to hire in mercenaries to do the job because he knew he didn't have enough soldiers of his own. He was one game away from succeeding in that venture - the financial side of matters. The last game – he was winning… and Mister Roden apparently took it from him on their final game.'

Tarra sat back. So, all of it was true – and Mister Roden hadn't even broken any laws. She smiled and relaxed.

And once the first part of DCC Keene's home visit was over and done with, the rest of it concentrated now on the immediate life and activities of Mister Nate Roden.

First, just to calm the still very concerned Tarra Browne down, DCC Keene confirmed that Nate was indeed alive and functioning and his future prospects were sound – but not yet could he be released from a hospital scenario. In fact, and here Tarra frowned, Nate wasn't even in the UK anymore. He was in a Switzerland hospital where his care was thorough and private, paid for by himself. Away from the madding crowd and Press attention. One of the things Nate Roden *ABSOLUTELY* did not want was for his name and face to become a national and international fixture on TV or newspapers. The success of his life, the gambling, relied upon anonymity when entering games where the identities of those whom he played against – either in actuality or by proxy - was not generally known – but *especially* by other gamesters. DCC Keene suggested to the enthralled group that Nate might possibly be going through minor reconstructive cosmetic surgery. She told them that when he'd dropped from the chandelier in Sasha's bedroom, his landing coincided with the loud and large explosion which not only took the back wall but swept everything else up in its wake – Nate and the dead gangster included. It took some strength of character for him to get himself up into the Lodge's attic.

For Tarra, the news was enough for her to laugh, relax and cry – this time from joy.

Her job done, DCC Elizabeth Keene stood, thanked the Beddoes family for their gracious welcome and prepared to leave.

As she exited through the door, she stopped and addressed Sasha.

'I believe you are due a visit, Mrs Browne,' she said. 'A Mister William Morton. He is a Lawyer.'

DCC Keene left the house and the Police entourage, which was now surrounded by children aged from 8 years up to 82 years, glided out of the quiet street and towards the County Station.

Sasha turned to Annaliza and her Husband. 'William Morton?' she said. 'Who on Earth is William Morton?'

*

MISTER WILLIAM MORTON

'I don't understand, Mister Morton. Why are we being offered this?' Sasha Browne was confused. Mister William Morton sat in the armchair previously occupied by DCC Keene just a short while ago and had just told her and Tarra that the home belonging to Mister Roden was theirs for the duration of their homeless period should they wish it.

William Morton had arrived an hour after DCC Keene and the Police entourage had left the area.

He announced his name and Profession. He was a Lawyer. In this instance, he was here representing the interests of Mister Nate Roden and had been given instruction by Mister Roden to make this visit and to speak to Sasha Browne personally and privately. Annaliza, Tarra, Patrice and Mister Beddoes made themselves scarce and once food and drink had been provided, the private conversation started in earnest.

The upshot was quite brief in content, Mister Nate Roden had considered he was, in part, at fault for the destruction of the Keeper's Lodge and wished to make some kind of reparation in the form of either allowing the Browne family to reside in his home for a period of time or to be allowed to take rooms at the best hotels in the area at his expense.

Lainey and Tarra were called into this meeting since it included their immediate future, listened in to the nice Mister Morton and what he was telling them, in pleasant tones, and Lainey thought he was sweet old man who had a nice voice. Sasha was confused by the offer as she did not see Nate Roden as being responsible and couldn't understand the extent of his generosity.

Tarra was more pragmatic. She alone, out of the Browne family, knew exactly what was on offer as she had been inside Nate's home and she was keen to make certain Mummy didn't blow the gesture out of the water out of pride or shame. This was not charity – well, not *just* charity – and she was eager for her Mother to accept Nate's offer because she knew staying at the Beddoes home had a very limited shelf life and the possibility of staying at a hotel was simply not viable. No room could be big enough to furnish the family which meant, at best, she would have a room of her own and Lainey would camp down with Mummy. Not a good deal. Lainey was of an age now where she was becoming more and more independent as well as becoming a woman and putting the two together could be an explosive mixture and while a separate room works in a family environment, it simply wouldn't happen in a Hotel.

Mister Morton went on: They would not need to pay rent or Council Tax, they would be given a vehicle for transport as their car was one of the fire's victims. They would be allowed to treat the house as their own and any concerns rising from their temporary stay would be passed on to Morton's Law Firm and all problems would be resolved at that level. He, Mister Morton, would be in daily contact with Mister Roden and reports of all kinds would be made so nothing could go amiss for any length of time.

It sounded too good to be true and Sasha, who had serious doubts about such a generous act and was genuinely concerned that the attack made by those men might bring about a follow up by others. Her concerns were addressed by Mister Morton who comprehended her concerns and it was Tarra who suggested a visit to Mister Roden's home so they could judge for themselves, as a family, just how sound the idea was.

Reluctant all the way from the Beddoes home to the Roden home, Sasha kept her worries to herself. They reached the front entrance and Mister Morton unlocked the gate fence.

'Do you know this place actually has an electronic lock somewhere around here which opens these doors. Only Mister Roden knows where that lock is and he won't share it with anyone. Not even me,' Mister Morton smiled. Tarra smiled as well. She saw her Mother looking at her and she shrugged – she didn't know where the lock was either.

The gates opened and what Tarra already knew for sure came as an almighty surprise to Sasha and Lainey. Such beauty, opulence, style and elegance – such a difference to the Lodge or even their former family home – no comparison.

Lainey screamed. She saw the wide-open area – the garden if you like – and ran across it and around the house. She saw the areas Nate Roden had provided for the local beasts of the Earth, the table with the scraps of food on it, the bathing pools, the hanging baskets from the trees to cater for the birds and the hives which housed the bees. The shrubs which flowered around the area lent floral beauty and Lainey ran around the whole garden yelling her joy.

Sasha saw the area where Mister Roden exercised and understood his fighting abilities more now.

The front door was opened – again with an electronic locking device attached to the side wall. Operated by Mister Morton, it looked rather like a phone dial with numbers and letters. A dialled code opened the door – "OPEN SESAME" - and they all entered the house. Tarra saw it exactly the way she had seen it for the first time and watched her Mother gazing, breathless, around the home. They were escorted around the house and Mister Morton explained why certain things had been developed to this design – Mister Roden's own design, Mister Morton said. Tarra, of course, already knew. He didn't like sharp corners or doors, or straight lines - everything was curves and rounds.

Less than twenty minutes into the walkabout, Sasha could see she had no choice but to accept the gesture from Mister Roden. She assured Mister Morton the stay would be only temporary – while they actively would pursue a home of their own – and he accepted her word on the issue. Tarra knew they would be staying here a long while – at least until Nate came back. And for her, maybe even…

The deal was done.

The two older adults then spent an hour with each other as Mister Morton explained the details to Sasha while Tarra took Lainey through the house again, at leisure this time, to give her a better understanding of what the full deal was all about.

And then – back to the Beddoes home. Mister Morton said his farewells and, for some reason, shook Tarra's hand and asked her if she was happy with the arrangement, as if her word was more important. Tarra smiled and nodded and Mister Morton then drove away. Tarra watched him drive through the lane and she waved as he disappeared from sight. Sasha saw it all. She said nothing.

*

The Browne family spent their final night at the Beddoes home before taking up semi-permanent residence at their new home. Sasha gave Annaliza a thorough description of the home they had seen and Annaliza promised her she would be around there first thing in the morning to see it for herself, sounding almost envious.

Lainey and Phillipa had their final slumber party with the other girls just to confirm their friendship had not been beaten down by the nasty men with guns.

Patrice talked long into the night with Tarra and though she did not broach the subject with her, knew exactly how this relationship with Mister Roden would turn out. She was happy for her friend.

CHAPTER 24
A YEAR PASSES

A lot can happen in a year.

The immediate consequences of the fight and the fire at the Keeper's Lodge meant media coverage, lasting some weeks, local attention, naturally, concerns from well-meaning friends and an appeal to assist the Browne's glide into their new life. At first, Sasha bridled at the charity which was thrust upon the family but accepted there was no malice intended and, in truth, had the same thing happened to any other family in the area she probably would have participated in the same act of assistance.

So – clothes were brought – household equipment such as computers for each of them – and at least a month's worth of provisions was delivered to them the day after they'd moved into the new home.

Annaliza, Patrice and Phillipa came to visit after a respectable period of time had passed – actually three days – for the Browne's to become used to their new surroundings. Patrice was agog. The place was like a fairy tale for Lainey to grow up in and Phillipa wanted to know why their house didn't have round doors and windows. Annaliza rolled her eyes at Sasha and told her she could see there may be renovations happening at chez Beddoes.

After a short period of time, Sasha felt it appropriate to invite the neighbours to the house for a long day's barbecue and frolics so everyone could see how well the Browne family had landed on their feet after the fire incident. Everyone marvelled at the style of the house and wondered how and why it would only be occupied by one person. Tarra said nothing to these comments.

Lainey continued with her and her friends slumber parties – but in the passage of time, they moved on from 12 years of age to 13 and now near to 14 years of age and slumber parties were slowly dropped and more mature parties for the teenagers became the new normal.

The media attention – quite active in the first weeks of the incident which then became mini frenzy when the revelation of involvement of international gangsters became the primary story. From a highly placed source, someone was brought in to help die that part of the story down and soon, the Browne's were left alone and normality followed.

After two months had passed, Edmund Browne eventually made contact and wanted to know if there was anything he could do to help his estranged family. Sasha just stared at the phone. He asked if he could speak to the girls and Sasha dutifully asked Lainey if she would like to speak with her Father. She paused, wrinkled her cute nose, shrugged her shoulders and then shook her head.

Tarra was also asked. She also paused – then stood up, took the phone from her Mother's hand and turned it off. Then she went back to studying.

In the time which followed, Billy mad a few abortive attempts to regain position in Tarra's life. He knew what an ass he'd made himself look and instinctively knew he was no match for this man Nate Roden. While his company was tolerated, he had enough sense to know he was a bust and gradually effaced himself from Tarra's world. He would not be missed.

Sasha did not actively make many changes to the house – knowing full well the family would soon be required to abandon it when its true Master came out from wherever he was residing at the moment and coming back home. For sure, he would not be tolerating three females in this house – no matter how spacious it was.

Well, Sasha told herself, maybe he would tolerate one…

The subject of Tarra's feelings and emotions regarding Nate

Roden only occasionally arose between Mother and Daughter. Sasha knew full well not to interfere in this matter. A Mother's desires and designs for a Daughter's future aren't always for the better. Her own Mother practically begged her to marry Edmund Browne for he was "a man of property and great authority in the City". Prestige, her Mother told her, meant a future secured – "You will never have to want if you marry this man" her Mother had told her. Even after the truth of Edmund's infidelity had been made known her Mother persuaded her to keep the marriage going – only standing down when the infidelity was joined by embezzlement and scandal.

What do I know? Sasha asked herself.

And Tarra did not press the matter. This home had saved them, the wonderful act of friendship demonstrated by Nate Roden – and the fact that it was his courage in the Lodge which saved her, Mummy and Lainey *and* the slumber-ites from certain death could not be disregarded.

And in truth, Sasha had no legitimate reason to even dislike or distrust Nate Roden. Yes – he was… a wanderer, a gambler, an adventurer. In the media stories which followed the incident, much of Nate Roden's life became widely known. He had travelled around the world, backpacking, and had come to the attention of the many different Lawful authorities in many of the countries he had visited. Another meet with DCC Keene confirmed he was widely known around the world he'd walked in and certainly well known by the Law in the UK.

If this was a fictitious character in a book, she reasoned, it would be considered romantic. A latter-day sea-faring Buccaneer who raided other ships for their boodle – but only to feed his people, a cut-throat Pirate who still served the English King at war with other countries, a derring-do outlaw on the side of the Angels helping those who could not help themselves. The TV and novels were full of characters like Nate Roden. She'd read many of them as a child. All enjoyable fiction…

But he was not fictitious and it was her Daughter who was enthralled by this… man, this Buccaneer, Pirate, Derring-do hero.

But a Mother can only do so much. Tarra was not a child.

And so, a year passed and life became pedestrian. Sasha was now in full-time employment, Lainey was enjoying herself in her new senior school and Tarra was working near Lowestoft in Historical Studies for a firm engaged in the 1,000 years progress of English Villages. No-one there knew who she was and no—one pressed her on sordid events.

Saturday:

Tarra was speaking to her Mother on the phone while placing scraps of bird food on the table. She had already catered for the hanging baskets in the trees, had filled the baths with fresh water which were now being fully enjoyed by the smaller birds. To her delight, the larger blackbirds stayed on the table while she placed the different kinds of foods on it – just as they had done when Nate did the same thing. They felt safe in her company, knew she was no threat and she fed them.

Sasha and Lainey were in Lowestoft. Lainey had managed to persuade Mummy she was really interested in the local theatre of that town and since her Aunt Caron and Uncle Kenny ran their own small dancing classes which would result in full theatrical shows twice a year, she should be allowed to join.

As it turned out, Lainey was a natural dancer and singer and not only gave good performances but enjoyed the assisting of helping her mentors teaching the other students.

Today, Saturday, and tomorrow, there were to be full dress and technical rehearsals for the show beginning on Monday. Lainey was to take part and was excited for this was her first real show with the Company.

'Yes, Mummy,' Tarra said, 'I've been in touch with the Catering Company and they'll be delivering the dried foods tomorrow. The edible stuff will come on Thursday, ready for the Dance Company after Friday night's performance. Yes – bus laid on and the tents are already here. Big party, big night. Auntie Caron and Uncle Kenny will be bedding down in my room and I'm in the main room with the older girls. Lainey has the whole reception area to herself and the younger dancers.'

She moved to the front of the area and dropped the remaining scraps around the ground.

'Give them my love and tell them I'm looking forward to seeing the show. Okay, Mummy, talk to you soon…'

And the call ended. It was at this point she heard a noise she had never heard before and looked around to see where it was coming from.

What she saw took her by surprise.

The front gates were opening. By themselves. A wheezing electronic sound had alerted her and now the gates were opening.

She wondered if Mummy had been playing a joke on her and had been making this phone call from just outside the gates. But how would she know where the secret unlocking system was located?

Then she wondered if Mister Morton, the wonderful Lawyer who had assisted them many times in the past year had finally found out how to open the gate doors via the secret electronic locking system.

The gates opened wide and the first thing she saw was…

…an Aston Martin car.

She stood still – mouth agape. Her breathing had moved up a considerable pulse. The car was the same – same model, same colour, but the registration was not the same. Different car.

Her eyes widened.

And then…

A lone figure walked across the front entrance and stood by the car.

A man. He was dressed in torn denims, a makeshift jacket, a pair of jeans, ripped. His arms were muscular, bare and tanned.

She stared. She walked, slowly, towards the front entrance, her eyes widening, her mouth open. She stopped a hundred feet from the opened gates.

She continued to stare. Her still opened mouth closed a little to form a smile, her eyes moved from wide surprise to warm recognition.

The lone figure did not move and she was too scared to walk further forward. Her excited breathing eventually slowed down to a normal beat.

And now she really did know how she felt about this man.

Now, she thought, how am I going to explain this to Mummy?

The End.

www.ingramcontent.com/pod-product-compliance
Lightning Source LLC
Chambersburg PA
CBHW020806310726
48969CB00002B/724